BEST CANADIAN STORIES 2024

EDITED BY LISA MOORE

Biblioasis
Windsor, Ontario

FIRST EDITION

ISBN 978-1-77196-566-8 (Trade Paper)
ISBN 978-1-77196-567-5 (eBook)

Guest edited by Lisa Moore
Copyedited by John Sweet
Series designed by Ingrid Paulson
Typeset by Vanessa Stauffer

Published with the generous assistance of the Canada Council for the Arts, which last year invested $153 million to bring the arts to Canadians throughout the country, and the financial support of the Government of Canada. Biblioasis also acknowledges the support of the Ontario Arts Council (OAC), an agency of the Government of Ontario, which last year funded 1,709 individual artists and 1,078 organizations in 204 communities across Ontario, for a total of $52.1 million, and the contribution of the Government of Ontario through the Ontario Book Publishing Tax Credit and Ontario Creates.

PRINTED AND BOUND IN CANADA

CONTENTS

Lisa Moore

~~~~~~~

INTRODUCTION

I peaked in grade nine. My finest hour was at fourteen, in a parish hall. I was wearing a feather boa and a fancy dress borrowed from a costume department, stiff, prickly ruffles that whispered in several languages every time I drew breath. More pineapple than dress. The heels didn't fit, one ankle strap kept falling off. The shoes made me lurch and draw myself up with each step. It was a gait, I imagined, that looked both deliberate and vulnerable. I swagger-stumbled across the stage.

The parish hall with hundreds of parents and siblings and kids from other schools in the audience.

Crowded, I'm saying.

The play was a play within a play. One of those. I rose from the audience, where I had been planted, to interrupt the "rehearsal."

I was playing the role of the author of the play. I had to strut my few minutes upon the stage because the actors and director were misinterpreting my words. Destroying my work. I had to berate them. Beseech them. Mollycoddle, harangue. Clearly, a part requiring nuance and sophistication.

The roar of the crowd when the curtains closed, it could have been hockey or a rock concert. Actually, there were no curtains, but the applause was thundering.

It was the thrill of convincing people of something. Making them believe. Making them laugh. Pay attention. The waves of applause. Attention is like static electricity, a tingling invisible pelt you can almost pat, or smooth down with the palm of your hand; it sends shivers. The eerie, ecstatic feeling of becoming someone else. Wholly lost and altered. In the rehearsals, the *real* rehearsals, I'd try saying the lines in different ways, shifting the emphasis from one word to another, so I could see how it changed the meaning, the cadence, the very prima-donna-ness of my character, the author.

Voice. What voice means in a story.

I am fascinated with how people tell each other about their day, the supermarket, the doctor's appointment, the parking ticket, or their whole life. The details they choose to include, more rhythm than content. The rise and fall of the voice, the speeding up and slowing down, the rush of life, and the lull. Breaking the radiant moment into smaller and smaller bits, Zeno's arrow, so that the simple exchange of a receipt for the groceries might become something that unreels skyward and plummets, a fishing line looping through the air with a narrative hook.

In fact, I was only onstage for a very short time. It was a small part, but there are no small parts. If Konstantin Stanislavsky had been in the audience, he would not have been impressed. He was definitely not in favour of forgetting the audience, as I had done, or of the actor forgetting herself. Yes, draw on your innermost feelings and sensations to create character, depend on interiority and memory, but don't get lost in the dream when there's work to be done. Arm flapping, or the pressing of the back of a hand to a forehead before swooning, say, or nearly falling out of your shoes would not have been the thing. Build from the inside out is the method.

But Laurence Olivier believed in building a character from the outside in, beginning with the costume, the makeup, the clanking sword at the hip.

How a character is both a building up and stripping down.

I am trying to tell you how I picked out these stories for *Best Canadian Stories 2024*. What mattered to me. Voice and attention, the way a character is always in flux, the culmination of what they noticed/didn't notice. Characters coalescing, simultaneously from the outside in and the inside out.

Impossible to find an expert who can define the short story. I bet even Alice Munro would have a job of it. Maybe especially Alice Munro, because writing a short story means you disappear inside it, spelunking into the depths with a bungee cord under your armpits to make sure you can be retrieved and get the hell out of there before you cross over to the underworld.

In a public discussion with Alexander MacLeod, one of Canada's finest short story writers, we tried to define what makes a short story.

I said, It's short.

Alexander said it was compressed. I wasn't sure about this, because I'd read novels where every sentence and word had been chosen with an eye to concision. And what is a story of any kind but the buildup of words?

But Alexander was suggesting, I believe, that the compression of a short story is a kind of alchemy, changes the very nature of the elements with which you begin.

Like I said, not easy to define, because writers are always trying to bust their way out of an understandable notion of form, working against the definition of a short story or novel to make something new. But I left the discussion convinced about Alexander's idea of compression.

A speedboat we rented with another couple, coast of Mexico, a snorkelling trip, a guide who knew a good spot. The man of the other couple, I can't remember much, except he seemed in a perpetual state of delight and disbelief about having this woman at his side. We'd stopped for lunch in a cove that had a family willing to put out a plastic tablecloth on a wooden table, four plastic chairs, under a thatched roof for shade, just off their own kitchen. Otherwise there seemed to be nobody else around.

They had both come through fresh divorces, this man and woman we'd been thrown together with, simply because we all showed up on the dock at the same time. They'd met each other on a dating site.

She was born in Ukraine, and spoke both Russian and Ukrainian, she said, and she was Canadian.

I asked her about the war in 2014, because this was in 2019, before the current Russian-Ukrainian war, before Covid, before ChatGPT (of course it can't replace us, it can't *create*), before the Convoy, before Trump was found with nuclear secrets in his ballroom. Before, and here I am guessing the future, he became president again, and from jail pardoned himself. Before *Roe v. Wade* was overturned. (I had been in a car with a dog, coming back from the vet. The dog had found a moose bone and it got stuck in her jaw. She couldn't close her mouth or drink, drool and shame; she hid from us. When we found her, we were afraid to remove it, because we might knock it back in her throat. But the vet plucked it out easily, and heading back in a snowstorm, everything white, everything erased, the dog shivering beside me, I heard about *Roe v. Wade* and cried. Cried with my whole face warped, like melted plastic, mouth open wide, as if it were stuck that way with a bone. Of course, that's not Canada, but borders can be as porous as limestone in a rainfall.)

Soon there was more lobster and crab and we had bibs, juices splattering, drawn butter. Our chins were glistening. I knew I wanted to write a story about this woman, but it was just out of my grasp, I wanted it, I wanted her in a story. Not *her*, of course, because even as I listened, I was making her up.

She had blond sausage curls, plump lips, perhaps her late forties, early fifties. But it wasn't how she looked; it was something about the *way* she was. Or else I was getting a fever. Because she seemed to shimmer, or the edges of her shone like cut crystal.

There was definitely an edge, everything bright and full of glimmer, the thrill that comes with meeting a stranger. Or: it was the way this couple were together. Or: the way they were with us. Or: the way we were with each other while we were with them.

She thought before she spoke, the things she said felt compressed, wise, lacking guile.

What makes a character magnetic is the desire of another character. That they are desired. The inexplicable enigma at the centre of us all. This is what the short story also has as its centre, a pinprick in the retina, a black hole, a bull's eye, the unknowable we chase after. Desire to know. As Elizabeth Bowen has said, character is plot.

And yet she was willing to reveal personal things, the way we all do with strangers. The way we spread ourselves at a stranger's feet.

I had the impression she had narrowly escaped something. A massive financial loss, an illness. Not fragile anymore but still tender. Interiority. The story was almost there, but no matter how carefully I listened, and how freely she spoke, I could feel it slipping away from me, out with the tide. He took her hand, for no reason I could see, in the middle of the messy lobster. And I noticed the ring. Big honking diamond. I'm getting to precious materials, forged under great stress. The story must contain all that's missing, the history of its formation.

The guide at the wheel, facing into the wind and sun. Then helping each of us over the beach rocks to the feast of seafood prepared by his family. He pointed out the crabs rapid on their dainty stilettos, the pointy claws that hefted the weight of their carapace over the round stones, lots of them riding in with the surf, weird and determined.

This snorkelling trip was four years ago. It was impossible to tell which details mattered. Her white patent leather sandals carefully picking the way through the slippery seaweed and beach rocks. He patted his tummy and said she had him on a diet. Then she asked if we were going to such-and-such an island. She said they had plans to go tomorrow.

She said there were walls all around a perfect pool of fresh water, and, above, a circle of the sky, as if made visible with a hole punch.

Actually, my last husband left me there, she said. Bull's eye.

She pointed in the direction of the island and I looked across the water, but the heat made a haze, the sea melted into the sky. I couldn't see any island.

We now believe the Gulf of Mexico, near the Yucatán Peninsula, was hit by an asteroid back in the time of the dinosaurs, and that's what killed them off. Imagine the sizzle when that thing struck. The tidal wave. The heat wave. Vaporization. Somewhere in Alberta a giant raised its head above the greenery, part of a tree hanging from its teeth, and *swoosh*. The beast was barbecue. Just bone.

There formed around the Chicxulub crater left by the asteroid what is known as the Circle of Cenotes. Caverns shaped from rainwater seeping into limestone. Eventually the roofs of these caverns collapsed and what remains is a magnificent freshwater hole, with high walls and, above, a circle of the heavens. Below, some say, the underworld.

This is where the woman of my story was abandoned by her former husband. There are over two thousand cenotes, or freshwater pools, the result of this asteroid, which was her heart, or my heart. And the cenotes might be understood as a kind of plot, or the shape of a story. A pattern of images that a short story can configure into a plot. Because a story is short, the pattern may be delicate, barely visible, wispy but there, underpinning all.

The big, splashy plot reveal: this Circle of Cenotes was discovered around forty years ago and is recognized, by some, as the mark of an event that caused life to be drastically reduced around the globe. An environmental mega-collapse.

And the authoress was apoplectic because her work was being misinterpreted. She had to be placated, fawned over. She bellowed and trilled and trot-faltered across the stage. For a minute she really believed she'd written the play, or at least what it would have been like if she had, she was caring far too much about what art could be. She was a figure of fun who could not quite be dismissed because she was running while staying still in those high heels, running to keep the story going, to keep the story from ever stopping. Provoking laughter that kept her upright, by demanding everybody take her seriously.

Later, with the snorkel and mask, the sandy floor dropped away from me and I lost my sense of how to be in my body, the sense of proprioception, where my limbs were and who was moving them. I had been lifted and dropped by a wave and the floor rushed back up and this is what I want a story to do, disorient, disturb, make everything certain uncertain, so the reader has to ask who they are, or who they were, and even where they were. A lungful of salt water instead of the air I expected; I nearly choked and was overtaken by fear, the unknown below. A veil of sand stirred by the current obscures, reveals. Get me back in that boat, she was reaching over the side, along with the guide, helping me up the ladder.

And the story, by Jorge Luis Borges, about the map that is so detailed it unfolds over the landscape in such a way that every fold and crevice of the earth is covered by the lines of the map that denote them. The map is exactly the same size as the landscape. Ha! The story itself is a paragraph long. Borges's story makes me think it's possible to cover every square inch of Canada in stories. Or the whole world really. I wanted this collection to stretch over a large body of land and contain as many voices as I could jam in.

Sometimes I chose stories I'd read though they hadn't yet been published, because I wanted rural voices as well as urban ones; I wanted voices that were new; sometimes I wanted stories that unfolded in the future. Stories about power, and lack thereof. I wanted stories that were not realism, because it seemed a supernatural element was required to get us out of the mess we are in; I wanted realism, because we need that too. I picked some stories that were funny, because laughter is radical. Funny, these stories, but wickedly serious. And stories where language was the material in the foreground, every word textured, sandpaper, silk, grease, goo. I was looking for the catalyst, the keyhole, the secret note, the cenote.

And beauty, because it shakes us.

The asteroid created a precious metal called iridium. Something forged by tremendous pressure, something incalculably compressed. Because such compression creates the indestructible, like a perfect story.

I read the stories in all the literary journals Biblioasis sent my way, as well as many online stories. I loved getting these boxes in the mail. I loved tearing through the stories. Each story a deep dive. I only read the fiction, but I've kept all the journals to go back and read the creative non-fiction and the poetry of the past year. This *Best Canadian Stories* series is itself like a cenote, a core sample, a mark of the years that we cannot really know the full significance of without hindsight.

What does it mean to gather stories after a year of writing, each year, for decades? I read about the asteroid and came upon the description of an archaeologist who found the fossil of a feather, twelve inches long, which he believed was preserved in the instant when the asteroid hit and sent out waves of ash and changed the air into glass, and caught all the flora and fauna mid-action, preserved in muck. Some of these fossils fell apart when they were uncovered, little brushes flicking away the dust. This is the passing of time and its traces; these feathers are stories. All the layers of life—the political, social, aesthetic, and spiritual preoccupations, and their connection to the history that shaped them, scrawled in striations of sediment, year by year, to tell us who we are and how we got here. A pinpoint on an axis of time and space.

The other fiction by Borges that has been an influence on this collection is "The Library of Babel," which is a library that contains every book ever written, including books that appear to be copies of a book, but with an error that sets it apart from the original and makes it something new. I think all stories stand on the shoulders of the ones that came before.

"When it was announced that the Library contained all books the first reaction was unbound joy," Borges writes of the Library of Babel.

It seems to me that the series *Best Canadian Stories* is a similar project.

Madhur Anand

INSECTS EAT BIRDS

Teach me something, demands Mr Woodrow in the Woodrow Southeast Asia Wing, and she obliges. The iridescence of the peacock's tail is generated not by pigments but by optical interference. The two-dimensional photonic-crystal lattices within the layers of barbules cause amplification or extinction of light waves—Bragg reflections, as in William Henry Bragg, she adds, because Mr Woodrow likes names, his own, those of other humans, and otherwise, *Pavo cristatus*. Slight changes to the spacing of specimen parts results in diverse appearances—more or less beauty, flee or fight stance, better or worse exhibit. Starling? he asks, and she answers, *Sturnus vulgaris*. It continues like this. American woodcock, tufted titmouse, et cetera, in the bistro attached to the hotel three blocks away. He orders *oeuf croustillant, fenouil croquant, crème et chips d'ail,* and when they arrive, a miniecosystem in an absurdly large and asymmetric white ceramic bowl, everything looks disgusting. She brings along a few skins from the teaching collection, and when she is no longer on public display, she arranges them across the impeccable white hotel bed. They excite her for reasons different from his, but the complexity of sexuality is not a new concept. The Kama Sutra includes diagrams on sexual positions as well as advice on how to teach starlings to talk. She lays out a good amount of diversity, *Scolopax minor, Baeolophus bicolor,* a skin for every mood.

*

A woman calls to ask if it is possible to taxidermy her cat after he is put to sleep. She answers that not only is it possible, there are people who do this for a living, but adds that it would likely not have the effect she seeks. It may make the pain of the pet's death infinite, and has she ever heard of "ambiguous grief"? Better to bury or cremate it, she suggests, and move on like the rest of us. She often gets calls not related to her job. She thinks it is because she is the only female-looking human on the institutional website and people assume she will be life-affirming. She is also the only brown person on staff. But female trumps brown in these matters. She is not incapable of nurturing, but she does have an ambivalence towards motherhood, or at the very least towards ova, and traces this tendency to bad luck and poetry. One time she picked up a *New Yorker* magazine left by a visitor in the coffee room and opened it randomly to a page with a poem on it. In the *New Yorker*, there are never more than two poems. What were the chances she landed on one that described an exact experience from her own childhood? In the poem, a girl is tempted by a couple of boys to bite into a small blue egg. It is almost Easter. The girl pops it into her mouth and the bloodied contents spill across her tongue. She will never forget that taste but it comes rushing into her mouth again now. She is not sure if it represents simple evil or misdirected karma. Either way, she had thought twice since then about everything offered to her that is supposed to be delicious. About mistaking something real and containing the potential of life itself for the risen Jesus manifested in milk chocolate. And she could not get over the cruelty of children.

*

These incursions or excursions with these visitors—too wealthy, too grieving, or otherwise in need of animal companionship—if not for them, she would remain in her office on Level Four Mezzanine getting bored to death by the oversights of others. An incorrect species name is entered into the online database VertNet, a skin is in the tray of an entirely different Order. When she explains her job, Ornithology Museum Specialist, to those outside the museum world, she says it is like being a librarian, but for birds, and then always has to remember to add that vital technicality, dead birds. Wayne is in the adjacent office. He wears a cowboy hat at all times. He is sixty-two and has worked there forever. He gets to prepare all the skins, which she knows is correlated, mostly to the cowboy hat. She can do skins, she even has her own collector number series, but she can count on one hand the specimens she has been asked to skin since she has worked there, and even then she must use Wayne's initials to enter them into the database.

*

She hardly ever sees the curators. They have no need to touch the skins. If they leave their luxuriously carpeted offices, knowing this decor attracts carpet beetles, it is to travel to some tropical destination for a collection trip. It is okay to say things like "it is what it is" in the real world. Birds eats insects. Curators get to travel to exotic places for good reason. Men get to do the skins for no good reason. But things can reverse quite easily. For example, she can open a drawer to find the feather fluff of a hundred white-necked Jacobin hummingbirds, as if the birds have flown around in there overnight having a pillow fight. In the case of activity, "mild" or "infested," found in a drawer, the specimens are wrapped in plastic and put in the freezer for a week or more. But one day a few African birds collected in the 1950s are gone, entirely consumed. Only the indigestible handwritten cardboard labels have been left behind. She dusts off the frass and puts them into another box for the archives and labels them *Labels*. She enters the data into the database: false negatives.

*

A revolving door at the public entrance opens to where god-sized cockroaches and rats live, the filthy outside. But things getting in is how passive diffusion works, and the pests eventually end up crawling all over their unrelated taxa. The electronic key-accessed freight elevator in the research collections area opens up to a poorly sealed roof with windows. She has found evidence of clothes moths in the vestibules on all floors and traced it to an infestation of a sawdust pillow placed at the bottom of the shaft to absorb dripping oil of the past century. It could be worse. There could be a dead body down there. There could be ghosts. Another time she found the remains of edible underwear in the corner where the *Fringillidae* are stored, the ignorance of student volunteers or a cruel joke by a jaded visiting artist. There are areas no one visits for days and there are few cameras. Staff leave their office windows open. It is a vulnerable place, the natural history museum.

The giant park across the street magnetizes migrating birds, while the museum is a magnet for dead ones, each with their respective north and south poles, invisible fields. It is a fundamental force of nature, and it is the early wet season, and she has done this countless times. Found almost-dead migrating songbird to rescue from decomposition. Birdstrikes against the museum windows, birds wanting in. She puts them out of their grief, and hers, by pressing gently on their sternums. Just enough to cause them to have a heart attack. She watches them take their last breath and puts them in bags to skin later and add to the collection under Wayne's collection number series. If the window is closed, and the species is a parrot, there will be feather dust imprints, a negative for someone else to witness. Whether the windows are opened or closed, there is only one possible outcome for them and us.

*

At first Mrs Woodrow tells her she simply likes to spend time behind the scenes, the inner research collections, but when she asks to visit only the turn-of-the-century South American sunbitterns on the top floor, she suspects intergenerational ecological trauma. By way of either expertise or wealth, they enter into their privilege, the filthy freight elevator. When they reach the top, the window to the roof is open, and a warm breeze enters the climate-controlled wing like a warning. They notice a half-smoked cigar on the ledge. Someone has expensive tastes, Mrs Woodrow says of the Arturo Fuente Don Arturo Gran AniverXario, with a Colombian accent, just like my husband. Cryptic birds display their large wings with patterns that resemble eyes when threatened, one of twelve species of birds that bait or lure to attract prey to within striking distance, Mrs Woodrow recites from memory of Wikipedia. She props the heavy elevator door open with the red brick placed there for other purposes. She puts the brand name cigar in her mouth and asks for a light. It moves from one female mouth to the other, along with the Latin names of birds. It tastes on the one tongue of broken eggshells, and on the other of salvation, but as these things were entangled long before they met, no one will say which is which.

Sharon Bala

///////////////

INTERLOPER

The post had been delivered while the Bells were out. They spilled through the door, Vanessa giggling and Clive nipping her earlobe with murmured endearments, only to be halted by the maid holding a silver dish of letters.

Pulling away, Vanessa plucked at the tips of her gloves. The maid, an old family servant, had known her from a girl, and Vanessa, still unused to the mantle of *wife,* felt self-conscious in her presence.

Another missive from your lover, Clive said, shrugging off his overcoat.

Vanessa snatched up the pale-yellow envelope and went straight to the nearest window, the hem of her coat swishing at her ankles.

The Bells were only two nights returned from honeymoon and all the new furniture—the winged armchairs and pedestal tables they'd got down from Paris—was scattered about, covered in sheets. Curtain rods leaned against a wall, the naked windows exposing the double room, with its handsome crown mouldings and bare wooden floors, to the parade of strangers on the sidewalk. At 46 Gordon Square the front door was vermilion; people could not help but peer in.

Unfolding the paper, Vanessa held it up to the weak February sun, and announced: Ginny is in London. She's to call at half one.

There was evidently more as Vanessa clucked and chuckled to herself. Clive flipped through the rest of the post feeling put out. He thought it preposterous that his wife and her sister should exchange correspondence so often. Even on honeymoon Vanessa had refused to miss a day. Just once, he'd snuck a glance and been chagrined by what he'd read. *Dearest Ginny. My own baby, I love you better than anyone in the world.*

*

Virginia had passed the two months since her sister's wedding in agony, grieving their brother Thoby and terrified for Nessa. Letters were insufficient. Always there was an anxiety that misfortune had struck in the intervening days. It was a relief now to approach the beloved old house, her heels a rapid metronome across the cobbles.

The siblings had taken the lease together, after their father's death. Freed from the patriarch's tyranny, the trio had moved to Bloomsbury and gleefully scandalized their relations. Nessa riding her bicycle to art college. Virginia scribbling away at stories. Thoby bringing his friends round for boisterous, convivial evenings that stretched till dawn. Even Clive's omnipresence at these gatherings, preening and chirping, fawning on an indifferent Nessa, had been mere irritation. For two providential years, they'd enjoyed domestic harmony. Until the twin tragedies of Thoby's death and Nessa's marriage had cast Virginia out.

Through the glass now she could see into the front room where Nessa's dear, familiar figure leaned slightly back, fingers scratching forehead in a pose of consideration. The Parakeet was next to her, his every gesture, no doubt, a grand ejaculation.

When the maid answered the door, Virginia heard him droning on about the suffragettes. She recognized his commentary from that morning's issue of the *Observer*. Clive was incapable of originality. Instead, he parroted the ideas of his betters, passing their opinions off as his own.

Virginia interrupted with a loud hullo and was rewarded by the sound of her own name: Ginny! And there came her elder sister, at last, flying into her arms.

Here you are, safely returned, Virginia said. She sank, feeling Nessa brace herself against the extra weight, and inhaled the indescribable scent of home.

Sometimes it frightened Vanessa, her younger sister's need, its tremendous, insatiable hunger. It had always been there, before their mother's final illness, before their father's demise, before the first bout of madness, before the last, three years earlier, when Ginny had flung herself out a window.

They rested, foreheads together, and Vanessa whispered: Are you well?

Yes. Now you are here.

The whole time she and Clive were on honeymoon, wandering the Colosseum, shooing pigeons in San Marco's square, painting the Seine, Vanessa's conscience had been trapped in England, worrying about Virginia.

Ginny held tight. She would stay here forever. Vanessa drew away and, linking arms, said: Come, give us your opinion on the new art.

Virginia scrutinized the drawing room. There was the grand mahogany table salvaged from the family home and she recognized the outline of the pianola under a sheet. But how peculiar it all appeared without their brother's basket chair, her own scattered books and teacups.

A man passing on the street slowed to take in the domestic scene: newlyweds setting up house and a scowling young woman in mourning black removing her hat.

Virginia studied this newly married Nessa, the high-handed tone she took with the maid, the worshipful gaze she bestowed on her husband. It was unseemly, this enrapture, this idolatry, as if he were a Zeus or Poseidon. Though surely not Adonis. Clive was no Adonis, with his ridiculous pipe and the distant hairline, long receded like low tide. What on earth should have attracted Thoby—and now Nessa—to this twitching lump?

What shall we do with this? Vanessa asked, gesturing to an oil painting. Inside the frame, a child dressed in blue leaned against the arm of a chair, his golden hair, and the plain green background, all of it done with casual brush strokes, the primary colours striking against the plain white walls.

Above the mantel, Clive suggested.

Isn't he very like the delivery boy from St Ives? Virginia asked.

Clive was irritated. Virginia always did this—brought up old reminiscences, as if to stake her claim. He opened a pouch of tobacco and watched the women together, making note of how Virginia reached for Vanessa, to stroke her arm or touch her elbow. How often, in this drawing room, had he heard them speak in their coded language, completing each other's thoughts, and coveted the instinct between them. He filled the bowl of his pipe and told himself: *I* am Vanessa's future. He had ruptured their unity and an ugly part of him was triumphant.

Vir-gin-ia. Clive pronounced the syllables of her name in a singsong voice and bounced on the balls of his feet with his hands behind his back. I have a present, he said. An obscure writer I've discovered. He brought the book out with a flourish. Pay no mind to the name. She is a woman.

Oh, George Eliot, Virginia said, hardly glancing at the cover. We've known her since the nursery. Show me your studio, Nessa.

They left Clive still clasping his gift.

Nessa had transformed the study. A sheet, paint-splattered, was spread over the floor. Canvases, in various states of completion, leaned against walls. A work-in-progress was propped on the easel. Nessa sprawled across a divan, pulling the pins from her hair while Virginia made a slow, admiring tour, discreetly spying her sister's reflection in the looking glass. Before marriage, Nessa had seemed unaware of her beauty, but now she was resplendent, all sinew and limb.

Your name should be Victory, Virginia said. Goddess of the marital bed. Even your painting grows more confident.

Clive is a great help. He is uncommonly receptive, Nessa said. You should show him your stories, Ginny.

Virginia flinched. You haven't let him—

Of course not. I'm merely suggesting.

Virginia crouched to examine a painting so she wouldn't have to see her sister's punch-drunk expression. Today it was all *Clive says* and *Clive feels*. Only a few months ago it was *I do wish Mr Bell would leave me be*.

But then Thoby had contracted typhoid and suddenly it was Clive, not Mr Bell, who was at Nessa's side. Everyone said it was grief that drew them together, but Virginia thought it was Thoby himself. Thoby was cleaved in two now—his childhood, and growing up, bound up with Nessa, his time at Cambridge, his formation into a man, rapid but truncated, entrusted to the Parakeet.

Vanessa opened a folder on her drafting table and gave it to Ginny.

Here is something, she said.

She had begun it in Paris, sitting at the open window in their rooms, admiring the Seine, remembering her brother on their last trip to Greece, how voluble he'd been as they toured the ruins, full of youth and vigour.

Virginia opened the folder. Thoby. In charcoal. The image so true it stole her breath. She touched her fingers to his hair, as if to brush it off his forehead. Nessa laid a hand on top of hers, then squeezed. He was the best of us, she said.

Virginia shook her sister's hand off. Weeks after Thoby's death they had gone and got married. Banished her to an attic in Fitzrovia, all alone to grieve.

*

Sure enough, the child was crying when they arrived, wailing senselessly like a ghoul, its wrinkled face red with fury. Virginia stood on the bottom step and listened to the Parakeet twitter as he carried things in. Cradle, bath, and perambulator—an alien constellation she felt ill-equipped to handle. Meantime, Nessa turned circles in the sitting room, rocking the baby in the cradle of her arms, the nurse in her orbit flapping useless hands.

How was the journey? Virginia addressed the question to her sister.

We shared a compartment with a vicar from Bristol, Clive replied, setting an easel down.

Yes? Virginia kept her eyes on Nessa.

Clive went out and returned with two suitcases.

He regaled us with his opinions of the Liberal Party, Clive said. They're ruining the country, you know.

Truly? Virginia said, finally turning to him.

Clive put his hands on his hips and said, Our only hope, as it happens, is—

He had to raise his voice over Baby's caterwauling.

—is to wipe out all the Hindoos.

How extraordinary, Virginia said.

Nessa was near tears as she paced, whispering, Shh, shh. Virginia returned upstairs to her bedroom. It was difficult to pretend the squalling thing was human.

Virginia had been in St Ives not five days when Nessa wrote to say they were coming, that Ginny must keep the double room because she and Clive anyway preferred their own singles.

Virginia had rented a townhouse, one in a row of six with elaborate brickwork and stained glass. The landlord's family—some people called Rouncefield—had cleared off to the third storey, giving her the run of the first two floors.

Her bedroom had a balcony with a view of the bay and Porthminster Beach. From here it was nearly possible not to hear Baby. She sat with her work—a review she owed the *Times Literary Supplement*—and tried to focus. It was late afternoon and the tide had retreated, leaving the fishing boats suspended high on the dunes. Spring here was grey but hopeful, the grass greening nicely, crocuses poking up out of the newly thawed ground.

Eventually, Vanessa popped her head in, the maid behind her carrying in the tea.

Now Ginny, Nessa said, pecking her cheek. Don't be cross.

Virginia said nothing and they sat together looking out toward Godrevy Lighthouse, black and white striped, an austere guardian on his lonely island. As children they had called it the Cyclops.

From an open window a boy screamed—in anger or in jest, Virginia could not rightly say—and an adult barked an order.

The Rouncefield brood, Virginia whispered, and their lodgers, all of them crammed into four bedrooms up there. They are forever thundering around.

Since arriving, Virginia had been dismayed by the noise and chaos overhead. When she'd asked the number of lodgers, Ruth Rouncefield had said three, then leaned in conspiratorially to add: None have had a bath in seven weeks.

Vanessa pressed her lips together, her laugh threatening to spew tea. Ginny, you are awful.

None 'ave 'ad a bath, Virginia whispered, mimicking their landlady's accent. Can you credit it, m'um?

The upstairs window banged shut and Nessa returned to her new favourite subject: Who shall Virginia marry?

Annoyed and feeling contrary, Virginia said: But what of my Sapphic tendencies?

Ginny watched her with that arch expression and Vanessa, disconcerted, wondered if it could be true. Her sister had changed in recent weeks, at times seemed a stranger.

But that should hardly matter, Vanessa said. Inversion is very popular these days.

I hate it, Virginia said. All the speculation and intrigue.

In truth Virginia knew she held no attraction. Young men wanted capable wives. Sturdy women like Nessa who could manage their moods and required little tending.

Vanessa broke a ginger snap in half. It was true she had been pressing the subject. She and Clive would not have come to St

Ives at all—every task was made monumental with tiny Julian—but for her fear that Ginny would grow morbid. Rattling around on her own, with only the happy sounds of family life overhead for company, how could she stand it?

What about Lytton Strachey? Vanessa asked. He is rather charming.

A raging homosexual—

From somewhere deep in the house, a child cried. Nessa paused, a finger on her lips, and cocked one ear.

The Rouncefield child, Virginia said.

But Nessa refused to take up the conversation until she'd satisfied herself that it wasn't Julian.

From the hallway Clive saw the sisters huddled like conspirators. He was momentarily confused about who was who—their posture and mannerisms being so much alike—until he recognized his wife's dress. He saw the child was not with them and wanted to go in. It was rare to get Vanessa on her own; Baby monopolized so much of her attention.

In the birthing room, Vanessa had barely noticed his entrance, so entranced had she been with the child in her arms. Propped against the pillow, she'd seemed aged in an instant, hair a fright, eyes bloodshot and the skin under bagged out. The room was rank and Clive had sweltered with his back to the fire.

Come and meet your son, she had said, and they'd made a cautious exchange, Clive afraid the whole time that his arms should fail him. Inside the blanket lay something unrecognizable. A bruised and wrinkled creature with a conical head.

Well old chap, he'd said, examining the wizened face. Well, Julian.

On the balcony, the sisters chortled and he felt like a voyeur skulking in the doorway. It was not, he told himself, that he did not like his sister-in-law. It was only that she bewildered him. In her presence, he had the discomfort of being watched. Virginia would wait, silent as a stone, hoarding his every word and gesture to use against him in an unexpected moment. She could strike with a shaming remark, phrased with so much elegance and wit it was impossible to take offence without losing face. Then she would sit appearing magnanimous, having given the gathering a nugget to thrill over (*You are too clever, Ginny,* Vanessa would snicker), while Clive, indignant, was bested.

Steeling himself, with a false hearty swagger, Clive entered the room. What are you girls gossiping about?

Virginia ignored him. There wasn't space on the balcony, yet the Parakeet insisted on hovering with an insolent grin. Why must he always come between them?

She said: You know, Nessa, this place is full of painters.

The light here is very fine, Vanessa agreed.

Eighty artist studios and not a single one to let, Virginia said.

Clive withdrew. It was as if they hadn't even noticed him.

*

Virginia, barricaded in her ensuite dressing room, sat with her fingers in her ears, trying in vain to construct a sentence while the Rouncefields stomped overhead. A door slammed and the walls shuddered. Virginia prayed they would perish in a freak accident or perhaps—as they tumbled and screamed bloody murder—at one another's hands.

The third-floor racket had been easier to ignore when she'd been able to work downstairs. But there were people everywhere now, underfoot and overhead.

Another almighty crash, a howling male, and Virginia lost patience. Vanessa, nursing in the drawing room, saw a blur of skirts and hair blazing out the door. Her instinct was to follow Ginny—who knew what mindset she was in?—but she was tethered to Julian.

Clive, returning to the house a couple of hours later, was glad to find his sister-in-law gone. How much nicer it was without her pacing above like a vengeful faerie. He was invigorated after a visit to the galleries and keen to discuss all he'd seen with Vanessa. He missed the days when she called him muse.

Vanessa, half dozing when Clive arrived, struggled to follow as he enthused about brushwork and composition, striding about the room with broad gesticulations. Julian mewled and she unbuttoned her dress. The worry that had nagged her all afternoon rose in pitch when she noticed sunset waning.

Clive was extolling the virtues of ultramarine, the pureness of its colour, when Vanessa interrupted: Ginny's been gone for hours.

The child was feeding again and Clive could see a stain spreading across its nappy.

Does he need a new...?

Oh, let him eat first, poor Mouse, Vanessa said.

She winced and shifted in her seat and Clive turned away. It was vulgar, the sight of the toothless child, with his dirty bottom, clamped on his wife's nipple.

Have you painted? he asked, fiddling with a box of matches.

Vanessa yawned without covering her mouth. Do see if you can't find her, she said.

Clive, his back to her, said, It seems a shame to have brought the paints and easels all this way.

It's getting dark. I don't like to think of Ginny lost.

He thought this unlikely but went anyway. There was no point remaining now she'd burst his happy bubble. On the beach he spotted Virginia's lone figure among the seaweed and wrecked sandcastles. She seemed vivid and enigmatic in the light of the moon.

Virginia, who had spent the afternoon trampling over the cliffs and pondering the novel she was writing, now inhaled great lungfuls of crisp Atlantic air. She dreaded a return to the house where Nessa and Clive would be doting over the cradle, a blessed family trio that left her cast out.

Near the shore stood a tower of stones, high as her knee. A child's construction that brought to mind long afternoons of imagination and industry with her siblings. The memories filled her with an unaccountable fury and she aimed a vicious kick. Picking up the stones, one by one, she began flinging them out to sea.

Or the house would be in noise and chaos, Baby wailing his heart out and Nessa at her wits' end. How foolish Nessa had been, to surrender first to Clive and now to the infant. She had a perverse compulsion to injure them, to break the charmed circle, as if in breaking she might find a crack through which to enter.

A squall blew off the ocean, portending a storm. A voice at her back hollered her name. It was Clive, making his way through the sand, struggling headfirst against the deafening wind. She bristled.

Come back to the house, he called, a hand securing his cap down. Your sister is worried.

The house, she said, when he reached her. She twisted her hair in one hand, to prevent it from flying in her face. The house is hateful, she said. How am I to think?

He saw the way she wrapped her arms around herself, staring over his shoulder, resolutely toward the lighthouse, and was surprised to find himself in silent agreement.

And see, even now she sends you, Virginia said. A spy.

Clive was wounded by her reproach. He was more exile than spy.

A gust flung her skirts, swirling them around his ankles, binding them together. Virginia was nettled. Why had Nessa sent an envoy instead of coming herself?

Leave me alone, she cried, running into the water. Oh, why won't you go away?

The tail end of a whitecap washed over her shins and the sea filled her boots. The tide receded and she stumbled. Is this what you want? she shouted as she sloshed away from him. To have done and be free of me?

Do you think I could return to Vanessa if I should let something happen to you? he yelled, wading in after her. Do you think she would have me back?

She trudged out and out and he was forced to lurch through the surf. An absurd slow-motion chase. The water was nearly to his waist when he finally caught up.

A wave crashed around them. The frigid North Atlantic. Virginia nearly lost her balance again and Clive, heart pounding, lumbered to reach her. His clothes were leaden. The lighthouse's long beam shone a searchlight on them.

Please, Virginia, he pleaded through clattering teeth. Your sister is anxious.

He offered a hand. She regarded him with a steady gaze. Then, picking up her skirts and turning back to shore, she said: She cares a nought for either of us. Nessa would have us both burned to cinders for a single day of her child's happiness.

*

Vanessa watched out the window, impatient, her darning in her lap, one foot rocking the cradle. Revived by a cup of strong coffee, she had finished Ginny's latest essay, a childhood recollection of their mother and older half-sister. Ginny's writing was extraordinary. It seemed only to improve, full of nuance and veracity, recalling the exact sound and texture of old memories.

Vanessa sat by the oil lamp, brooding over thoughts of her mother and half-sister, years dead. Gloom descended and an image rose in her mind. Three poppies, a medicine bottle, and a teaspoon. Still life. A suspended, underwater feeling. She longed to be at work, her smock covering her arms, the brushes in hand. But the prospect of unpacking the easel, searching out her tools, was overwhelming. And anyway, the daylight was long gone.

The sky began to spit just as she made out two shapes hurrying toward the house. She braced herself for the inevitable bickering. Instead, they came in a pair of drowned rats.

What has happened? Vanessa demanded, half out of her chair.

It's only a bit of sea water, Virginia said, wringing out the end of her skirt into a puddle on the carpet.

Ginny's hair hung in sodden ropes. Her cheeks were bitten by cold. Yet how lively she appeared. Clive too, though shivering at the fire, seemed pleased with himself. What adventure had transpired?

Julian's finally knocked off, Vanessa said, and took up her darning. If they would not tell, she refused to interrogate.

Virginia knelt by the rocker to inspect her nephew. He was swaddled up tight, eyes shut in two creases, tiny chest rising and falling. In these moments he could be very sweet, she thought. But the amount of business that had to be got through before one could enjoy him was dismaying.

He is the image of Thoby as a baby, Vanessa said.

For Vanessa, her brother's death, the wrench of it, had been worse than anything else. But then Julian had been born and his existence obliterated all else, even, mercifully, her grief.

Already he has the same mannerisms, Vanessa said. The same staring eyes.

Clive put a hand on his wife's shoulder. When she spoke like this, he thought he might love the child as she did.

Oh, they were great pals, Virginia said, glancing at Clive from her crouched position. Thoby and Nessa, romping like puppies. They had their own secret language.

Virginia rose and took a seat by the fire. Reaching up into her skirts, she unrolled one wet stocking, then the other.

Until Ginny broke into our twosome, Vanessa said. Weaseled her way into Thoby's heart with her big green eyes and her charm.

There was never such a thing, Virginia told Clive. Everyone of course has always loved Nessa best.

*

Did you gad about with the locals? Clive asked. When you used to come here on holiday?

Oh no, Virginia said. It was only us Stephen children and the dog.

Bundled in jumpers, they stood on the slipway watching the boats rowing into the harbour and nursing their bitterness. At breakfast, Clive had folded the weekend edition of the *Times* and congratulated Virginia on a piece she had contributed. Upstairs, Baby squalled and two sets of feet hurried across the floor.

Succinct and incisive, Clive said, raising his voice. I haven't read anything so good in years.

Virginia showed him her copy of Delane's biography which she was to review next.

Vanessa thundered down the stairs, a harried scowl on her face. Can you two please keep your voices down?

Oh dear, Virginia mock-whispered as they buttoned their coats. Mummy is cross.

What is the point of having a nurse? Clive wondered now as they loitered in the cold.

It was a bright, overcast day, the sky more white than grey. Gulls wheeled in shrieking, hungry circles while men repaired nets and negotiated on the wharf.

Summers here were a reprieve, Virginia said. Kensington was so bleak. You cannot imagine.

She gazed behind them, toward the rise of houses leading to the cliffs, and he knew she was hoping to glimpse the old villa.

There is another family there now, she said. Renters, I suppose. I spied through the gate and felt quite a ghost.

There was something vulnerable in her unguarded face and he understood for a moment the inclination that made Vanessa want to protect her.

Let's go into town, he suggested.

They took Bunkers Hill, a narrow cobblestone lane that inclined. Local children wound past them. Women yelled to each other from open windows.

Mr Joyce has smashed it all up, Virginia said, a hand on her hat, as they turned onto Fore Street. What a novel should be, the form it must take. He has thrown tradition from the window. I should like to achieve something similar.

St Andrew's steeple loomed over the chimneys. A woman huffed past with a wheelbarrow, forcing them to walk a little closer together.

You are not destructive, he said, though he thought in fact she was.

It is simply the order of things, Virginia said. She pointed to two children who ran past with pails and shovels. They build their forts and castles, she said. And then the tide comes in and washes it all away. Destruction is natural.

They turned into the market and skirted around a boy at the corner bellowing: Murder in St Erth! Read all about it!

Get away, get away, Virginia shooed when he held a newspaper out to her.

In Hamlyn's General Store, Virginia stood in the doorway and shook sand from her skirt. There was only one other customer, a local woman with her basket, gossiping with the shopkeeper.

Em'ly, her name was, the woman said, wrapping her pumpernickel loaf in a gingham cloth. Strangled by her lover.

A slip of a girl, the shopkeeper agreed. She used to come in with her ma. Not a day older than sixteen, if you ask me.

The woman unclasped her reticule and counted coins. Her parents. To think how they found her.

Sat up in a chair, the shopkeeper said, extending his hand for payment, as if she was alive.

Excuse me, Virginia spoke up, and Clive coughed into his fist. Virginia's patrician accent rang through the shop. Are you *quite* finished?

The woman, rotund and rural, frowned, affronted.

Lord how the working classes enjoy their melodramas, Virginia said when they had left.

And they joked about it all the way back, taking it in turns to mimic the shopkeeper and his customer.

At the house, Vanessa was hidden behind a broadsheet.

William Hampton, she said, lowering the paper to her nose as they walked in. They say he was her fiancé.

Then they've caught their man, Virginia said. There will be an end of it, at least. She scooped Delane's biography off the table and went upstairs.

You've been gone for ages, Vanessa said, offering her cheek for a kiss. What did you speak of for so long?

This and that, Clive said. We made ourselves scarce as requested.

He reclined in the wingback across from her and removed his pipe from his pocket.

Lytton Strachey's latest, for one, he said. Have you read it?

Vanessa was silent and he felt her eyes on him as he filled the bowl of the pipe, sealed the pouch, and rolled it into his pocket.

It's no use playing Cupid, she said finally. Ginny has Sapphist tendencies.

Clive looked up. How astonishing.

*

One morning Virginia lifted her breakfast plate and slid a notebook across to Clive.

You may read this if you like, she said. It is the first chapter.

Vanessa was upstairs with Baby. Her feet beat a steady rhythm back and forth above their heads. Clive tapped the spoon against his boiled egg, cracking the shell. The moment felt profound and he wished to say something appropriate. But Virginia took a slice of toast off the rack and wrapped it in a handkerchief. She stuffed cotton wool in her ears, pushed back her chair, and said she was going to work in her room.

When they walked in the dunes the next day, he was shy of

her and ventured only to say that he thought it exceedingly good though perhaps a bit verbose. At first she seemed to shrink, but two days later she said, Yes, I see the truth of it, and showed him a revised passage, all the indulgent lines excised out. After that, she divulged everything, as to a confessor, insisting: You must be the surgeon. Cut away what isn't wanted.

He admired her work ethic. She was writing a review of Delane's life for *Cornhill Magazine* but begrudged every minute, yearning instead to bash away at her novel. Even on their rambles he could tell it was all she thought of, their most frequent topic of conversation.

It is a powerful feeling, she said, stepping smartly on a rock. These godlike powers. She conjured her hands over the water, swirling them above the minnows in the shallows, and said, I can control my characters. They are my puppets.

She made a striking figure balanced on a rock at low tide. Nearby, two children with net baskets hunted for crabs.

What is that little girl thinking? she said. There are whole worlds inside each of us.

This was what she wanted to capture. The life of the mind.

Give a sense only, Clive said. And allow the reader to intuit the rest.

Yes. That is it, exactly.

Her eyes remained on the children as the girl skipped from rock to rock singing a song of her own devising. Virginia's gaze was not doting, as Vanessa's might be. Her expression was shrewd. She was collecting every nuance and gesture to resurrect on the page. It came to him that Virginia could never be maternal. He could not imagine her in such dependable mundanity. She was earnest about her work in a way, he saw now, Vanessa would never be.

Writing is foremost, Virginia said, taking off her straw hat and turning her face up to the sun that had broken through a cloud. To have a quiet room, a pen, a blank page. A still mind. This above all is contentment.

*

At the house, Vanessa wandered through the empty rooms wishing for company. Julian was asleep. The maids were in the back garden, clipping laundered nappies on the line. Even the Rouncefields had been lured out of doors by the sudden sun.

Her sister's bedroom was open and Vanessa went in. The blinds were pulled up and the acorn that trailed at the end of the cord, swayed by the breeze, scraped back and forth across the floor.

Stepping onto the open balcony, she closed her eyes, turned her face to the day's bright warmth, and listened. Gull cries, horse hooves, rolling buggies, the rare motor car.

She wondered where Clive and Ginny had gone off to. She had been short with them earlier and now she was sorry. She was not surprised by Virginia, who was possessive to the last, but Clive's lack of interest in their son hurt her. Even now, as she stood here, revelling in her liberty, a part of her wanted to hurry to where Julian was sleeping and touch his silky hair.

Leaning against the railing, she scanned the street below. If she were here, Ginny might affect their father's gruff voice and say, Now what shall we speak of? But of course Vanessa would have nothing to say. The evening before, she had come down from bathing Julian to find the two of them in the drawing room, speaking naturally for once instead of sniping. Vanessa had left her copy of *Les Liaisons dangereuses* out and they were debating the author's intent.

What do you think, Nessa? Ginny had asked, and Vanessa was forced to admit she had barely begun and kept muddling the characters. She'd fallen into the striped loveseat and pushed the hair out of her face, only to notice there was vomit on the front of her dress.

They had carried on until dinner, Virginia arguing the novel was a tirade against the aristocracy and Clive holding forth on the amoral plot. Vanessa could contribute very little and was listening the whole time for Julian's cry. She knew she was becoming banal and could do nothing about it. It was like watching herself, a person called Nessa, from the outside, and having no control over her actions.

*

I see nothing of her, Clive said, huffing uphill through the tall grass. The child commands all.

She has taken completely to motherhood, Virginia called over her shoulder. There she basks like an old seal on a sunlit rock.

They were tramping up one of her favourite windswept coastal paths, jewel-toned ocean on one side and gentle meadow on the other. They paused at the summit among the yellow gorse and purple heather. The view was immense: an unbroken stretch of rugged clifftop, aquamarine waters stretching beyond the horizon.

I no longer know her, Clive complained. She never paints. She doesn't read.

A falcon swooped overhead. Farther out at sea, kittiwakes called to each other.

Virginia frowned. I can't seem to get at Nessa first-hand.

Clive draped his jacket over his arm. He dabbed his handkerchief on his forehead.

Motherhood and marriage, Virginia said. I hope these are not institutions that ever pertain to me. Then she turned and strode off.

Here is a woman, Clive thought, watching her sure, quick clip.

Under her straw hat, her hair was coiled in a bun. He longed to undo it, run his fingers through the wavy masses. No guilt accompanied these thoughts; the stranger at home was not his wife. His wife had abandoned him for an interloper she called Julian.

He was a step behind and grasped Virginia's waist, hardly knowing what he was doing, acting only on instinct. She turned, her mouth an O. Then her expression relaxed into knowing.

Virginia's reflex, at suddenly feeling a man's grip, was revulsion. But then she spun, saw Clive's face, and thrilled. Butterflies flitted. The ocean crashed and foamed against jagged fingers of land. The path was deserted, the whole world empty but for them.

This is right, she thought. Exactly right. That they should remain here like this, their faces so near without touching. Seeing Clive from this vantage, these freckles on his cheek, the mole by his left ear, the long, ungainly nose, she felt at one with Nessa.

You are changing everything, he said. You are the sea, eroding all the old ways.

I am capable only of shocks without any true lodging in your lives, she said. Nessa has all I should like to possess and you have her.

They had never stood this close and Clive had the pleasure of feeling her body—so solid between his hands—as familiar and mysterious. Those well-known, sensuous, rosebud lips.

He leaned in, closing his eyes, and Virginia wrenched away. Turning to the ocean, one hand against her side, she covered her mouth.

God forgive me! Clive exclaimed. Virginia, forgive me.

She shook her head, mute. He could not see her face. What on earth had he done?

Virginia, please, he begged. What a thing to do. Heed none of it.

Her heart pounded. For a moment she'd been at peace. Now she touched her breast and felt the knife turn there. It was the old dread again. To want and want but never have.

Don't, she said. Don't speak. Let us go back.

At the house, Virginia went straight to Vanessa's bedroom and shut herself in. Clive was in the horrors. Pressing an ear to the door, he heard a murmured voice, Virginia sobbing.

*

Next morning, Clive was alarmed when Virginia descended with her suitcases. There was an early train to London and she wouldn't hear of being accompanied to the station. A few days remained on the rental, she said, and Nessa and Clive must see the week out.

Vanessa, uncharacteristically complacent about the change in plans, offered a passive cheek for her sister's passionate kisses. Virginia even fussed over Baby, pronouncing him a darling, a poppet, a little prince.

To Clive she was reticent. I've been a bore, she said, offering a handshake. Say you'll forgive me.

After she left, Clive was antsy. He stalked the drawing room, pocketing his pipe off the mantel, twirling the tassel of the curtain, getting in the maid's way as she tidied.

What did she mean by it? Had she no feeling, no sentiment? Had he been merely a distraction against weather and monotony?

Vanessa cradled the child with one hand and held a broadsheet with the other. Clive kept his eyes on the arabesque-patterned wallpaper and away from her barred breast, heavy and pendulous, the dark veins, and the baby's greedy mouth.

A thousand people turned up for that poor girl's funeral, Vanessa said. Hundreds and hundreds had to wait outside.

Is it right to read such things in front of the child?

Oh, Clive. Be sensible.

She sat up as she said this and the motion made him forget himself and look at her. The baby's mouth lost its grip and Clive caught a glimpse of an elongated nipple. Jerking his gaze away, he spied a hardcover wedged between two cushions.

He's to be hung, Vanessa said, disappearing behind the newspaper. This William Hampton.

Clive slipped his hand into the sofa. Delane's life.

In Bodmin Jail, Vanessa said, and planted a lingering kiss on Julian's head.

Virginia's book, he cried, and hurried to the door.

Vanessa was startled. She made to stand, then remembered the baby and shouted her husband's name. The newspaper slipped from her fingers, pages scattering across the carpet, out of reach.

I'm going to the station, Clive called, already on the street.

*

Virginia boarded and wrapped herself in a shawl. She felt hollow. Her thoughts flitted between Nessa and Clive, the moment he almost kissed her—he nearly had, she was sure of it—and the hours she had spent in Nessa's room.

She had sat at the foot of the bed and sobbed, desperate for Nessa to wake, to heap coal in the hearth, and say: Now Ginny, what shall we talk about? The past, the present, the future, even who shall Virginia marry? She would have agreed to any subject. But Nessa had remained sunk in a dream, steadily snoring.

Sitting with her temple against the cool glass of the train window, Virginia touched her waist and recalled Clive's hands on her. She closed her eyes and felt an emotional convalescent.

He would be speaking with Nessa now. Or filling his pipe while she fussed over Baby. They would have returned to the secret rhythm of their marital life while she sat here alone.

Down below on the platform, Clive scanned the windows. The conductor, with his neat hat and uniform, strode the length of the train calling: All aboard. All aboard.

A pernicious mist hung in the air, settling on everything, dampening his face. Clive spotted Virginia's long nose in profile, her heavy-lidded eyes. He hollered her name.

Virginia turned at the sound of her compartment door sliding back. A pink-cheeked woman hefted her carpet bag and hat box onto the shelf overhead then sank down with a great exhalation. Nearly missed it, she said.

The whistle blew and the train rocked into motion. The woman sat across, their knees nearly touching, but Virginia didn't mind. She liked the anonymous, fleeting intimacy of a rail journey. Clive jogged and thumped on the side of the train car with the flat of his palm. Above, her temple rested against the window. He saw again the rosebud mouth. VIRGINIA.

The woman rubbed her handkerchief on an apple. There's a man wants your attention, she said, rapping the glass with a knuckle.

Virginia gaped at Clive and he waved the book at her. The train quickened its pace, the rods moving forward and back, the wheels chugging round. Clive ran, an unnatural act. Virginia grappled with the window. The shawl slipped off her shoulders. On the platform, people goggled at him. Mist had turned to drizzle. He sped up, wet hair pasted to his head.

Clive! Virginia called.

Half her body was out the window. She reached a hand to him. He sped up, heart pounding with the effort, the small volume held tight. They strained for each other, Clive, thoroughly drenched now, sprinting alongside the train, all the passengers watching. The horn blew an ear-splitting whistle. He felt her grasp the hardcover and he let go, relieved.

My book, she said.

She laughed a brawny guffaw and to him it sounded musical. They held each other's eyes. He had to tell her. He did not care who heard.

Virginia, I—

A stone caught underfoot and broke their gaze as he tripped and went face first, crashing hard on his knees. When he lifted his head, dazed and on all fours, the train was speeding away. The fabric of one trouser leg torn, sharp pebbles digging into his palms. Her car long gone and a line of gawking strangers passing overhead.

Gary Barwin

~~~~~~~~~

GOLEMSON

There is love in me the likes of which you've never seen.
—Kenneth Branagh, *Mary Shelley's Frankenstein*

Night. I was waiting on a bench. On the sidewalk. In the fog. Toronto, Eglinton, near Dufferin. Outside a music store, its window filled with accordions, lurid red plastic trumpets, and an LP of *Que Sera, Sera,* leaning against some maracas. It was a fitting theme song for the students who passed through the little back room, taking lessons with Pasquale, at least in terms of the uncertain melodies they produced with their nervous, ill-prepared fingers. But kids—who knew what those fingers were capable of now? The future's not ours to see, after all. It may possibly be filled with skilled accordionists.

But night and fog. The music store mute. He was walking down the street, moving between clouds of lamplit luminosity and obscurity. Wearing a dark suit and a bowler hat. Like Magritte or the men in his paintings. And like me.

Kidding. In a bowler hat, I'd look more like an aging droog. He moved toward me, with no kind of expression on his face, but I saw he was a form of regret made manifest. One of my many regrets. Usually they're not so dapper.

My golem.

I hadn't seen him for years. We'd lost touch and, in a way, I was surprised I recognized him. Surprised he was still alive. I didn't think golems could live so long.

We had been close once. Twins. Lovers, of a kind, even.

No. We never were. I know nothing of his viscera. I do not know if golems can love. Or if they can make love. With another golem. With anything. All that clay. Might gum up the works.

It's said that, like Adam, we're all born as golems. Guileless mammal-forms. That misfortune shapes us into the complex humans that we are. But I've met some breadboxes more capable of love than many of the misfortune-moulded walking Freud couches I've encountered.

"My dreidel," I'd joke. "I made you out of clay."

But how do you make a golem? I didn't know, so I googled it. It is said that you harvest a bathtub's worth of clay exhumed from a grave by a riverbed and fill a body bag. You take it home and form a colossal three-dimensional gingerbread man with your mortal hands. You knead the shapeless husk to near-human shape. You are tender and stern. You do this at night while weeping, praying while drunk.

Then you write the name for God on the skin of a woman who has died in childbirth, skin the span of a baby's chest. Or you ask for and are given a hymen on which you write *Elohim*. You write a *Shem,* a name of God, and a magic formula on a piece of parchment, a slip of paper—it could be a Post-it Note—and place it in the golem's mouth. You write "אמת," *emet,* the Hebrew word for truth, on its forehead. When you wish to undo the life of the creature, the creature who was only a certain kind of alive, you erase the first letter, aleph, leaving, "מת," *met,* the Hebrew for dead. If you do not know Hebrew, you write something else. You free-write. You edit. You take the name of God from its mouth. Again the creature becomes the bed of a river, is the earth only, can be used to make pots, or coffee mugs, or terracotta tiles.

How had I made the golem?

Clay. Amphetamines. The Hebrew I remembered from my bar mitzvah.

A kit ordered from the internet.

It was a mess the first time. The second time also.

I threw the clay over the fence.

He'd come to me in the night. I woke and, before I opened my eyes and saw him, I knew he was there, standing silently by our bed, a massive presence, a dark shadow in the dark. Wearing a dark suit and a bowler. A nice touch, I'd thought.

Mary was in the bed beside me. We'd been married for six years, though we'd been together for thirteen, having met at university when we both lived in the Annex, on Brunswick, just off Bloor. We tried to have children, but eventually our doctor had determined that, in terms of procreation, I was a Peter Pan, a feeble warbler in a choir of perpetual boys. The few swimmers I had were dog-paddling splutterers, only good for show.

"Will I ever be able to have a child of my own?" I asked.

"Unlikely," the doctor said.

We tried anyway. Each month a ritual of waiting, of hoping, praying, of temperature-appointed times, of reassurances. Of discussions of options.

There was a month when we had thought Mary was pregnant. Hoping against hope. Mary was late and she had a feeling, a kind of murmuration behind her ribs. Blood cells turning in a slow saraband, or maybe it was too much smoked meat, too much coffee, an anxiety–hope blend. We'd been trying for so long. We'd made tomato sauce and soups together, had made bread and family meals, as if through this ritual we could transubstantiate our relationship into a living thing, a viable zygote that would divide and divide and divide into our child Zeno's paradox, the arrow finds its mark, the rabbit overtakes. We would make more cells in the world and the world would come into greater focus, a kind of higher-resolution pixillation. Our story would become more vibrant, luminous. Moving. Happy.

But as we worried and hoped, I was increasingly turning into a kind of clay myself, my cells joining, not dividing, becoming large simple shapes. Cellular goons. At one point, I gave sperm to the doctor to be concentrated, centrifuged, boiled down like maple syrup, syringed.

Syringe. I remembered when I was a child in an Irish hospital ward. Rows of starched white sheets, metal-framed beds. A large needle stuck into my upper thigh. The needle still in, the starched blue nurse replaced the syringe with another and again emptied it into my muscle. I'd been given a first-day-of-issue cover, commemorating John Millington Synge. I thought it said John Millington Syringe. His shaggy-dog moustache and expressionless face.

"Are you happy?" my wife would ask.

It was then that the golem appeared beside my bed, silent, shadowy, dapper.

My golem. I made you out of clay.

Was the golem happy?

It was then I ill-advisedly quit my teaching job without telling my wife, even though we had no real savings. I imagined myself a sad sack in a Tom Waits song, heading west with a suitcase and a back seat full of bourbon, looking for cheap hotels in which to write a mixture of despair and out-of-focus faith. But really, after I quit my job, I just stayed home, became silent, and slept during the day. My marriage ended. My grandfather used to say, *"Der oylem iz a goylem"*—"People are fools." And I was people.

For years I thought I saw my golem walking down the street, in the booth at a restaurant, in the passing lane beside me on the highway. I'd kept watching for him, waiting. And then I got an email. It was from the golem. All caps. Typical. I didn't take it for internet shouting but as an ironic dig at the simple preschool sensibility of the average golem. My wife—my ex-wife—had had a child. Unto her a son was born. Apparently, the child was his. I imagined their late night coupling as if it were a folk tale and they, in the rain and fog, in a graveyard, had come together, an elemental and preternatural force. Hundreds of years ago, as if it had to be so. The cracking open of gravestones and of things as they were. I saw her thin hands reaching around the incredible clay hulk of the golem's shoulders, gripping, leaving scalloped impressions, like a child's squeezing fingers in a kindergarten craft project. The golem like the swaying of an old tree. His face wasn't peaceful; rather, I'd say, unperturbed. From a different time, a character in a legend following the story he knows to be written for him with quiet resolution and little emotion.

But it wasn't like that.

"I MADE THE CHILD," his email said.

Again, an opaque night. A story. Under the crow limbs of a dark tree, he did agitate his fertile horn until his seed was free.

Lightning striking the oak in a Jekyll and Hyde moment the instant of the golem's grounding. Glass vials like vacuum tubes hidden under the black wing of his cloak. And then he rides to town, a Headless Horseman, with his satchel full of jism.

I assumed that Mary hadn't planned on being the mother of the golem's child. I thought of that creepy yet surprisingly beloved kids' story where the mother slinks across town, sneaks into her grown son's bedroom to hold him and sing of her love, and imagined the golem silently crushing the screen door handle in his fist and letting himself in the back door to Mary's kitchen, Mary stretched out on the living room couch, her nightgown hiked high in the summer heat, bottle of her customary sleeping pills beside her. Stalwart, silent, unblinking, the golem solemnly approaches. The golem had a syringe. A turkey baster.

But then my story fades. It was not the story he wrote in his email. Yes, he arrives and stands before her in the summer heat, but then he touches his big fingers to her slim face. The golem large as an armoire. She smiles. He leans down, a hummock come to life. He kisses her forehead. She feels the cool coils of his lips, the low rush of his breath. His eyes are endless, filled with desire. To be human. To be tender. To love.

He would lie with Mary, would be lithe Romeo to her delicate Juliet. But almost-human that he was, he could not. Yet Mary would lie beside him after, butterfly fluttering through the great forest of his body. They would join. Would share life. Would create it, as the golem was created from the unpromising mud of earth. Life would be created by sharing life. Their life. His forehead pressed against hers, imprinting it with the word. *Emet.* Truth. *Met,* death, always there within the word, but also, marked on Mary's skin, its mirror image.

The golem and Mary, from his sample, did join gametes, both male and female, and so did cause the spring. And I, distant, absent, my words telling another story.

The child, the golem said, was named after me. Kidding, he said. It wasn't. They named it René, after Mary's father.

When I'd finished reading his email, I'd responded immediately.

"Golem," I'd said. "Congratulations. To all of you. And—since you seem to have some experience in this sort of thing—grant me, if you would, this kindness."

All the golems, from those in the Bible to those in Reb Loew's Prague, were Claymation palookas with no more wit than a brick. But they had life. Sometimes, a golem is created out of longing, ambition, failure, and a need to know that you are somehow real, that your ministrations and hope may affect the world. But sometimes, too, in time, a son can create his own father, a golem too, can create the writing that created him. A kind of pearl writing the clam into being. As I wrote him into life, or at least wished it, so he would write me.

And so in the Toronto fog, we met at the hour and location he suggested. Midnight at the bench, outside the closed music store.

My golem was carrying a small box, a dented green metal cooler, held to his chest in an embrace. Protecting it, as in a mother-and-child painting. I was both disturbed and relieved by what was likely inside.

"I have it," he said.

"Don't spend this all in one place," I said, and handed him an envelope. "Really," I said. "Don't."

And then he continued down the sidewalk, past the 7-Eleven, the library, the mattress store, and into the night. What was in the box? A corned beef sandwich? A donated heart? A taxidermy squirrel dressed as Napoleon, little tricorn hat pinned between its ears?

I opened the box with apprehension. I felt a cloud of cold on the back of my hand. Inside, an envelope. I pulled out the slip of paper with a sense of inevitability and dread.

"אמת."

Billy-Ray Belcourt

ONE WOMAN'S MEMORIES

There are a few portraits of Jesus in Louise's home. In all of them, Jesus's gaze is both sincere and unspecific and, because of this, it evokes whatever the onlooker needs it to, but always with deep seriousness. Today, it reflects back Louise's sombreness. Because it feels good to have one's emotions reflected back to you, she hasn't ever taken down the portraits. Jesus represents for her life as a kind of quality, something not equivalent to biography though certainly bound up in it. It is like motherhood, Louise has thought once or twice. To be a mother is to represent for someone else life as an abstract quality.

Louise isn't a practising Catholic, but she does believe in heaven and the transmutability of suffering. Louise might say that suffering doesn't exist for the sake of itself. She wouldn't use the word *suffering,* however; it'd go by the name of something more identifiable, like a headache or fatigue or joint pain or, more ambiguously, "the past." Typically, Louise has treated the past with ambivalence. The past is an empty house; we can wander through it but we don't need to drag furniture inside, she thinks. It might seem ironic, then, that her walls are cluttered with photographs of her parents and siblings and late husband but especially of her son, Paul, tracing his childhood to the near present. But what really is a photograph? A photograph is a way of representing the past that doesn't bring it to life. A photograph gives shape to history, allows us to fashion a landscape of feeling at the expense of other more ungovernable feelings. A photograph is a ladder that goes backward in time—we can push the ladder away whenever we want. In other words, a photograph can obscure the past as much as it can illuminate it.

This afternoon, the house is silent and cold. Louise is sitting on a large floral couch beside a telephone receiver. The receiver is grey and hard and unattractive in the way that all new technology seems ugly to Louise. A green light glows from the receiver. She picks up the phone in one hand and dials Paul's number with the other. She never has to think about his number; it exists inside her like a heartbeat. They have had countless conversations over the phone, but Louise continues to be struck by how close his voice sounds when they speak. It is as though they are talking from across a room and not across hundreds of kilometres and a quarter of a province. The dial tone drones on and on. Paul doesn't answer. Louise considers leaving a voice mail but decides against it, not wanting to appear needy or to disrupt the rhythm of his day. After she hangs up, it occurs to her that she is lonely. She looks over at Jesus again. She reassesses her feelings. *Yes, I am lonely,* she confirms. *It is winter and I am lonely.* Louise doesn't tend to consider herself a lonely person. That would mean confronting aspects of the past she's ignored. Lately, though, the past has welled around her in all its glistening clarity.

Against her nature, she wants to discuss the events of her life. It is a new urge. She has lived through so much and yet has discussed so little about that living. Maybe it is because a new century has begun and she still feels like a part of the preceding one. She belongs to the twentieth century, she is indivisible from it. However much longer she lives, however greatly the world changes, that fact will remain unchanged.

People don't really expire, Louise thinks. People die, but even in death they continue aging in crooked photographs along a wall in someone's house.

What does it mean to be a living monument? The question hovers around Louise all night.

*

It is the middle of February in the Subarctic. Snow has fallen over everything like history. The aspens around the reserve lost their leaves months ago. Now their branches jut out frailly toward the sky, as if in prayer. The blue is so expansive it is unreal; it is the opposite of human consciousness. Louise is shovelling snow off the path that leads to her car. Her car has been idling for thirty minutes to melt the ice covering the windshield. She is sweating despite the frigid temperature. She pauses to wipe her forehead. She looks over at the forest. It elicits in her a kind of sympathy, not the cruel kind, but rather something akin to closeness. She identifies in both the forest and herself a state of wavering. That is, like the boreal forest, she too has endured season after season of loss. Without foliage, the trees don't tremble. This morning, it is Louise who does the trembling. It is as if some part of the winter she is currently living through has embedded itself inside her. Does she have a use for her sadness, which feels so much like winter? Yes, in that it is also a homeland, a place where she is never in exile.

*

The grocery store is normally a twenty-minute drive east, though in snowy conditions it can take twice as long. Louise's winter tires are several years old; their treads have flattened considerably. And so, she is moving slowly along the icy highway. Since the death of her husband, the car has gone mostly unattended to. They hadn't actually married, though she thinks of him as her husband all the same. In Louise's mind, marriage is for the young. When they met, he was a non-status Indian because his mother had married a Métis man (this gender-biased clause in the Indian Act wouldn't be amended for several more decades). It was Louise's mother who advised them not to marry. It made total sense, it was a kind of Indian common sense at the time. When Paul was born, he was given Louise's surname as well. Minor manipulations of colonial law shaped everyday life. It was too late when her husband's Indian status was at last restored in the late eighties. It seemed silly to them both to have their love, which was already so instilled with truth, codified by the government.

This is what she is thinking about as she pulls into the town in which she does her shopping. The town is what some historians call a "railway town." As the railway was etched into the prairies like a tear, thus creating "the prairies," this town came into being. For decades, there was a de facto mode of segregation in place. White families tied first to homesteading then to the railway and then later to lumbering in the area ruled the town. Indigenous peoples came and went, because colonization meant that they were implicated in the settler economy, but they rarely lingered. Horror stories abounded. People kept away. Louise is a part of this history, as are her loved ones, though she has never thought to describe it as racist. The idea was that it was simply the way things were, which is, of course, a function of racism.

In the grocery store, Louise puts more into her cart than she needs. Some white people stare at her rudely, but she doesn't notice. She runs into a distant relative in the produce area and they catch up for a few minutes. She desires a fuller conversation, but their location runs counter to that desire. It's as if everyone is listening in. She promises to stop by the relative's place later in the week and they part ways. When she returns to her car, it's become frigid inside again. She blows into her hands and listens to the radio while the heat blares. It's a song she's never heard before.

The drive back to the reserve is more slow-going than the drive out. The snow is heavy and affecting Louise's visibility. About fifteen kilometres from her house, she pulls onto a dirt road and puts the hazard lights on. She grips the steering wheel after putting the car into park. She closes her eyes and rests her head against it. The heat cascades over her face. She remains this way for a long time.

*

When Louise arrives home, she checks to see if she has missed any calls. She hasn't. She will have to wait until the evening to call Paul again. He lives in Edmonton where he works in student support services at the university. He is the first person in their family to have earned a post-secondary degree. When he convocated, Louise sobbed in her seat in the large auditorium. It marked for her a subtle break from history. He would live a better life. It was a thought undercut with the whole of a generation's hope. As Paul rooted into the city, built his better life down south, fell in love with a Cree woman from a nearby reserve, he grew distant from his parents, from the north of his childhood. Louise wonders how it is a son and a mother cleave apart; it betrays what she knows about being a person. The cleaving was so gradual and mysterious it was almost as if it were in the end an inevitability. Suddenly, her son had become inscrutable. Her grief over this inscrutability feels so private that she doesn't give it outward expression. Perhaps this only adds to the air of disconnection between her and Paul, Louise thinks. Does she wish she had had more children? Sometimes. Mostly, though, she wants to undo time or to live the same life over again. To make small adjustments that would, of course, change everything.

She looks at the photographs on her wall, at the derelict ones of her father. He was a quiet man; his large stature was its own kind of statement. He was born years before any of the towns along the lake were even imaginable. He predated the railway but came after the beginning of a Catholic missionary presence. He had memories of the signing of Treaty 8, on the eastern shores of the lake, as well as nightmares about being unable to leave the reserve without the permission of the Indian agent, but he never spoke about them to Louise. He didn't talk much about himself. Not many of his generation did, Louise observes. They lived through land loss and famine and the inception of the residential school system. They were the first set of parents who had to endure the seizure of their children. Louise thinks about the reserve today and shudders at the thought of it being suddenly emptied of children. Children, in a way, are from the future, she thinks; they ensure futurity. Twice, Louise's father considered enlisting in the Canadian army to fight in Europe. To do so, he would've had to be enfranchised, to give up Indian status. Some Native men were doing so, perhaps with the dream of escaping the violence of colonization. Something in her father knew this dream was an impossible one, that Europe would only plunge them into a different kind of violence and return them to the old one if they survived. He had to defend his own children, his own people, he decided.

They had lived on the same expanse of land until he died from heart disease. Louise used to say that he had died of a broken heart. The metaphor consoled her, but it was, in a sense, also true. The heart was the first of his organs to falter under the pressure of so much structurally induced trauma. Louise thinks about him all the time. She felt close to him her whole life. He helped build the house she lives in now. Sometimes she touches the walls as though to do so is to touch him. It is an act of mourning. More than that, it is how she collapses the past into the present. It is a way of staying alive.

*

Later, Louise at last gets Paul on the phone. After they exchange pleasantries, Louise tells him she'd like to discuss her life. She doesn't want to ignore the urge, to allow it to dissipate. She is already tired of waiting. Paul doesn't understand.

"What do you mean? Did something happen?" he asks, concerned.

"No, no, nothing happened," she says. She laughs gently. "I want to talk to you about my past."

It is a foreign sentence. Neither have heard anyone utter it before. It occurs to Paul that he knows very little about his mother's past.

What he knows is limited to images, brief anecdotes, old family jokes. He feels a pang of shame about this state of unknowing.

If a mother is a shape of unknowing, then perhaps a son is a bit of dying light. It is never that simple, of course.

"I'm listening, Mom. You have my undivided attention."

She does. He has no plans this evening. His girlfriend is out with friends.

Louise laughs again. She's nervous. She doesn't know where or how to start. She fidgets with the cord in her right hand.

"The summer after my last year at the mission," she says finally.

Paul hasn't heard that word in a while—the mission. It is the colloquial way people refer to one of the residential schools on the shores of the lake. Louise was forced to attend one for the entirety of her primary and secondary schooling. Some years she wasn't able to leave the property. Other years, luckier ones, she was able to visit family on weekends and during the summer. The fact that it was never certain when she'd be able to leave was its own kind of torture. Louise hasn't said much about her time there before, nor will she tonight.

"I had befriended a girl named Sue from a reserve to the east," she says. "We were inseparable. It was more than a friendship, more than sisterly. We were all we had. We were all we had of one another. We vowed to go on an adventure right after we left the mission. It was all we talked about. It saved us, in a way. We wanted to traverse the valley to the north, maybe even follow the river back to the mountains in the west. Most of that was dreaming, naturally. What ended up happening was that we would meet halfway between our reserves and find the water from there. We would sit in the lake and talk about the world as though it was what was owed to us. The love I felt for her was familial but also more than. We held hands sometimes and something in me ached when we did. I didn't know that two Cree girls could fall in love. I didn't think to ask Sue if she loved me. That possibility was unthinkable, really. We were still caught in the shadow of the school, but we tried to live as though we were free all the same. We spent our summers that way until I met your father."

"Did you ever talk to Dad about Sue or did those feelings ever come up later?" Paul asks plainly. He isn't sure how sentimental he should be about the conversation.

Louise thinks. She can hear Paul's breathing, his soft inhalations.

"No, it never came up. He was as straight as can be."

They laugh. Paul thinks the same could be said about him. Maybe it is even an inherited defect.

Louise continues, "My attraction to him never wavered, so I didn't think too much about it myself, to be honest. It wasn't until recently, now that I'm alone so much, that I've begun to reminisce about Sue. We lost touch sometime in the eighties. We wrote letters back then. Simple dispatches about our lives. They didn't seem special then, but I sift through them nowadays and feel a great deal of nostalgia. In one of them, she told me about her children, all ten of them. Her family must be multiplying, getting bigger and bigger."

This remark is imbued not with envy but with a tinge of melancholy. Paul hears it and he winces. He thinks about how unpresent he's been, about how alienating his unpresentness must be. Why has he stayed away? Truthfully, he isn't entirely certain. Life on the reserve is too compressed, he thinks. He feels that he begins in his mind and not in his body. To be on a reserve is to be beholden to your body in a way that he struggles with. At the university, he deals with policy and numbers and ideas and emotions. It is his job to ensure Indigenous students are supported and make it to the end of their degrees. He aspires one day to go to graduate school, to maybe even do a PhD, teach at a local college. Nothing in him necessarily yearns for northern Alberta. Sometimes he feels that this is a kind of personal failing. Worse, a social one. When he's especially self-loathsome, he feels that he is failing to be a good son as well as a good Indian. Visiting the reserve is a duty he's happy to carry out; he enjoys spending time with Louise. It is in the city that he feels most at peace, though.

"Now on to your father," Louise continues. "As you know, we met when my aunt married his uncle. I thought he was the most handsome man on the reserve..."

As she makes this comment, Louise glances over at a photo of the man. It is in black and white, he is wearing denim and a cowboy hat; his aura of goodness is clear, she thinks. After all these months, she can still detect a glimmer of his goodness. She still feels good by extension.

"I knew I would be with him for as long as humanly possible. When I had you, when we moved into this house, I knew I didn't need anything else. I would be happy for a long time."

Something suddenly feels heavy in both Louise and Paul. The subject of her husband and his father hadn't come up since the funeral in the fall. He died of a heart attack in the night (a family of Indians with bad hearts isn't uncommon). Louise woke and he didn't. She always thought that she'd depart first, so his death fractured her frame of reality, made her feel lopsided and blurry. Ultimately, they were both overtaken by the blurriness of grief, just not in the same place. To grieve apart from one another is itself a minor tragedy.

"When he died," Louise went on, despite her voice breaking, "I had to figure out how to continue to live. I had done everything with him. We had never slept in different beds, not once. We were together for so long and yet I still wanted more time with him. He was what I knew about the world. Without him, I feel lost, I don't have as sharp a sense of purpose anymore."

Some people don't take to the singular *I*. It isn't anyone's fault.

Paul thinks about his father. He was loud and energetic and he loved fishing and gardening. He regrets having missed out on so many of his father's last days. No one knew they were his last, but he wasn't around anyways. He doesn't talk to the dead. It doesn't come naturally to him. He wishes someone had taught him how to. Instead, he's listening to his mother on the phone, picturing her, visualizing her small body; he hasn't seen her in person since Christmas. For the sake of the holiday, they didn't talk about the past or the dead. Perhaps they should have. Perhaps that task is always more urgent than anything else, he thinks. Maybe it is all they can do.

"I suppose the main point of this conversation is that I miss him so much," Louise says.

"I miss him too, Mom."

Silence. Wind rustles outside both of their windows. It's expected to be one of the coldest nights of the year.

Paul continues, "Hey, maybe you could come stay with us for a while. We've got plenty of room. A big house and just two of us in it. Yes, please do. I can come pick you up whenever."

Louise considers the proposition. Through the window she can see that the snowy field across the road is shimmering. There are many weeks of winter ahead but at least the earth is shimmering, she thinks.

Louise's sense of self is tied to where she is. She can't leave the reserve. All her memories are here. Gratitude washes over her as she realizes this.

"I'll think about it, dear," she says, and this satisfies Paul.

"Okay, Mom, I'll call you tomorrow, how's that?"

"I would like that," she says, before saying good night.

*

After she hangs up the phone she goes to her bed to lie down. She is tired; it's been a long day. For a moment, she swears she can smell her husband. His earthy aroma is whirling around her once again. It disappears as soon as it appears, but she understands just then that he hasn't left her entirely.

Sometimes to remember is enough, she thinks, and then she says it out loud.

Xaiver Michael Campbell

PITFALLS
OF UNSOLICITED
SHOULDING

There is a scientific name for my sensitivity to smells. *Olfac-tophilia* or *osmolagnia*. You can take your pick. Aromatic, musty, sweaty odours make me stupid. I am an active pheromone sensor. Sniff sniff. Smiles. But sometimes it's sniff sniff, yikes.

"These hot guys will be the death of me." I eased my aching body onto Latoya's massage table, my head melded into the pre-heated cushioned surface. Latoya's new studio was across from the harbour. The open window let in a crisp, salty wind that broke up the stale August heat that had blanketed the city. We were more than halfway through the new year and I was still making the same mistakes.

Latoya laughed as she pulled on my neck. Her hips brushed the flourishing fig tree pot in the corner of her office. The pads of her fingers put pressure on the left side of my neck. It sent spasms through my fingers. Her target? The muscle between the scapula and proximal humerus. My inflamed, tense, and agitated subscapularis, to be precise. No one was happy to see me back on this massage table because of a man.

"They just smell so good. It is absurd. I should be studied; I am willing to donate my body to science if it means that others won't get hurt by their innate uncontrollable impulses." I was a grown man acting like a boy with an underdeveloped prefrontal cortex. I scoured Latoya's fig tree for signs of new life.

*

I wasn't always like this, and it wasn't every hot guy that smelled like wonder. There was a hot guy once, the original hot guy, who I wanted to love me. He was all hair. Tufts of jet-black coils, like my afro, covered his limbs. I wondered if he conditioned his whole body. And could I do It for him sometime? He smelled like cuddles on a cold, rainy February day. He could fix me and help me gym my way to a killer ass. My mother would be forced to comment less on my pancake-like derrière which I inherited from her.

It was an otherwise mundane day in 2016. I swam 2 kilometers in the pool first thing in the morning. Went to all three of my seminars. Had a lackluster lunch with the friends from the Dairy Queen value menu. Library sesh, then gym, followed by a meeting with my writing group. This was the first year I decided to give "being a writer" the ole college try.

"You'll be living in poverty," my friends chimed in when I published my first short story. "Can you pay your rent with that?"

I lived in a cheap apartment on Cookstown Road across from the dingy Peter Easton Pub, which provided ample content for stories. The ceiling above my front door sagged about an inch over most people's head. Being vertically challenged, I was unfazed. Everyone smoked in my alleged non-smoking apartment, so calling the landlord was not an option. A sudden rent increase caused more strain on my finances. Finding my person could lead to a rent share situation. Though I would feel more accomplished if I could afford to live. The gym was included in my tuition; I went every day.

The original hot guy ran to lift the barbell off my chest. He placed it on the two silver holing poles above my head that the barbell rested on when not in use. I sighed, being almost at failure. When he parted his mop of arresting red box braids, his long, curled black lashes pulled me to his glossy brown eyes. I breathed him in deep. Tried not to smile as hard as I wanted to. He brushed his hair behind his ears to reveal a face I wanted to wake up to forever.

"You should," he offered, unsolicited, as if interrupting my workout wasn't enough. He trailed on and on like the comments section of any YouTube video.

I was irked from his first "You should," but he smelled like my future. Unlike most men who *hombre escuela*—what I and my friends call mansplainers—there was an added ounce of hypnotism imbued in how he mansplained. It made me wet and humble. He assumed I was weak, and he was here to rescue me. For some reason, on this non-descript day, I was ready to fuck with that. When I first moved to the city two decades ago, people thought I was a scary thug. Ladies crossed the road to avoid me, though they'd never admit it. Some of them being on the road to church and all. Problem was, sometimes the church was on my side of the road, so they'd have to cross back over. My black skin overshadowed the pastel knee-high socks and wrist purses I donned.

"You good, man?" His chipped right canine was picture-perfect. Did it hurt? Did he notice right away? Was it too late to find the fragment to ever reattach?

"I'm good. Thank you." I sniffed deep. Fresh blueberry muffins. How could his smell keep getting more yum? He stood even closer now. If the powers that be had shown me his face and then I got crushed by the barbell, I would have died happy.

"You should spread your hands a little wider when you grip the bar." The original hot guy put his fingers over mine and guided them to the gritty bar's smooth ring. "This is where you want your fingers to be."

I knew that.

"Try it." He smelled like he was worth obeying.

I took a deep breath, and I did as he said.

"One." He groaned. Clapped twice. "Two. Yes, bro." He clapped twice more. After the third, he took the bar and rested it on the two silver poles. He rubbed my shoulders as I sat up on the bench.

"That felt…" I breathed deeply. In and out. In and out. "Amazing. Thank you." I heard myself and didn't know if I was acting or not.

His eyes widened. He rubbed his palms together as if he had solved world peace.

I was acting.

"I'm Zev."

I already knew his name. Zev. I knew a Zev once that was Jewish. One could even say Zev was a Jewish name. Zev. Ze'ev. Hebraic for wolf. Finally, a real-life application to knowing Hebrew outside of Torah study with the Rabbi and chanting during Shabbat services. The front desk girl had given me his basic info when I first noticed him last week by the cable plate towers. Zev hogged both cable machines to do chest presses. His fro was stuck to his cheeks and the back of his neck. I loved his fro. I loved his red box braids. I loved versatility in a man. I never imagined he would ever lay a hand on me. This was a meet cute we could tell our future kids about as we broke challah over the Shabbat table. My mother is not ecstatic I want to marry a man, but she would be a little less upset if I brought home a nice Jewish boy. Was he Jewish? The front desk girl hadn't given me that answer. Would he convert? Zev. I could only hope.

"I'm Martin, nice to meet you." My tired and awkward outstretched hand met his curled fist.

He showed me his chipped tooth again as his lips opened into a smile. All thoughts were wiped from my mind.

When I walked through the gym's blue painted archways the next day, Zev's red box braids were knotted atop his crown. That was such a hot guy move. In my mind and heart, I curtsied toward him. In reality, I walked straight by Zev to the water cooler. I focused on the green fabric poking through my sneakers, pulling my big toe back into my shoe before he noticed. He smelled even better today. How was that humanly possible? Zev put his hand on his hips and tapped his left sneaker on the floor. Gold laces popped against his purple shoe. He swayed his hips until they met the vertical pole on the squat bar.

Was this all for me? I walked towards him to find out. It was. Was HaShem rewarding me for observing the Sabbath so diligently the past two years? Maybe.

"Let's do some legs."

I complied, forgetting whatever workout I spent the morning planning; I found myself in front of Zev blocked inside the squat rack. No complaints.

Zev squatted behind me for each rep. His shorts climbed up his legs until his bulbous thighs protested. I imagined how safe I would feel cuddled between those legs. I stepped back towards him.

"Easy," Zev cooed into my ears.

Maybe not HaShem, I thought.

The next day we did chest. With the end of each rep his chipped-tooth smile waited patiently to meet mine. I could do this with him until Earth combusts and we all burn. Did he want to? Not burn, of course. Did Zev want more than the continual serendipitous meet-ups at the gym?

The day after was a rest day. I needed it. Zev called and said we should keep moving. We lapped Quidi Vidi Lake thrice in pained silence. Then Zev kneeled by the brass statue of the rower. Was he going to propose? I hoped so. Instead, he squeezed ropes of green liquid into his mouth from his oversized orange water bottle.

"That's enough for today b'y. Give me a ride home? I'm wiped." Zev didn't look tired. I didn't think he tired. The smirk plastered across his face told me he stopped because he thought I was tired. I was, but I was tired from before we even began.

The car radio stayed off. I didn't want Zev knowing I was listening to "I've Got to See You Again" by Norah Jones and thinking about him. The last thing I wanted in his head. Any world where there was a Zev-and-me romance existed only in my mind's eye and the stories no one reads. The pile of rejection letters on my nightstand had only grown between January and March.

Zev had no trouble filling the air. I learned he has been a townie his whole life. He didn't want to go to university straight of out high school, so he did a personal trainer course at Good-Life. After six years of that, Zev went to university for HKR so could get into the physiotherapy program at Dalhousie. I tried not to look over at him as he licked his top lip between senten-ces. He smelled ridiculous and I wanted all that ridiculousness all over me.

Zev looked at his large, deep-brown, wooden front door. He lived in a new row house on Bond Street. It was not a sin-gle-family dwelling. The developer must have known one of the landlords on city council. It was too tall for anyone's liking. Very skinny. Of course, he lived here. Zev zipped his green jacket all the way up before opening the car door. The cool air rushed in. It was late March, the island's version of spring, winter 2.0. "You should try protein powder. Put some size on you. Come in, I'll make you a shake." It didn't sound like Zev was asking. As I shut the car door, I wished it was a vegan protein powder. Lactose allergy. Worse than any mere intolerance. I wasn't in the business of denying him anyways; I was a chicken with its head cut off.

Red brick walls lined the inside of Zev's house. A contrast to the bland beige vinyl siding on the exterior. The front door opened to a series of doors. Uninspired hotel-style abstract paintings hung beside each doorknob. A quick dark corridor led us to a sunken living room. Brick walled. A plethora of pot lights sprinkled throughout broke up the dungeonous vibes. It smelled like the radiators were melting. This was not what I thought the inside of this place was going to look like. It felt like a bad attempt at sophistication. Zev lived in this extra-tall monstrosity for which two perfect homes were sacrificed to make way for the first condo on the block no one who lives on the street could afford.

I walked closely behind Zev, his shoulders spread wider than usual. The kitchen was at the end of the living room. Zev immediately threw two green aprons into a basket. There was no hiding that Starbucks green. Did he moonlight as a barista? Did his parents help with his rent? Which Starbucks location? I don't drink coffee, but we all know I would chug back a venti double frappe caramel macchiato espresso if Zev handed it to me. How much was his rent anyways? We could share it. I was beyond ready to get out of my dilapidated hovel. The whir of the blender broke my trance. Zev handed me a white Styrofoam cup filled with purple goo. I was glad I couldn't see my own face; I hoped I wasn't drooling.

"You should drink it quick." Zev slammed his empty cup on the counter. He grabbed the blender like he was starved and poured round two. "Come on," Zev crooned.

I drank it; I shouldn't have. Milk. It triggers an immediate response as it coats my esophagus and travels south. Unmistakably dairy. Wretched. Yet beautiful. I was too enthralled to check the ingredients in the powder.

Zev squeezed my shoulders. "Attaboy. I'll see you round. Thanks for the ride. I gotta crash, bro." He walked towards the front door, I reluctantly followed.

I turned the keys in the ignition grinning. It felt like a decent enough date/hang/whatever. Severe belly rumbles pointed to whey protein or modified milk ingredients. I turned on Norah Jones to drown out my rising anguish.

Zev missed the gym the next week and the week after that. I called. Nothing. Texted. Nothing. Did he really exist? I tell everyone he took an actual piece of my heart with him. Every hot gym guy now has a way of getting me to do stupid things, to follow their stupid unsolicited advice. They don't even have to try very hard. Or at all. August makes five months since I have seen Zev.

*

"A little suck, but you'll start feeling better. And breathe. Deep breaths. Best August, hot like Oaxaca." Latoya enunciated the name of the Mexican city like a true snowbird.

I funneled air into my body through my nostrils until my belly was twice its size, lifting my body off the table a pained amount.

"Deep breaths and relax." Latoya lowered her neck to the open window. Stray strands of newly dyed burnt-orange hair were glued to her sweat-speckled forehead. She rested her head in her armpit and pushed all the coloured stray hairs towards her floppy bun. Latoya had been my massage therapist long before Zev. Her fig tree was just a baby no one thought would survive Newfoundland. We went to the same gym. I ran to Latoya after Zev and I did chest for the first time in March. Zev's compound sets sent literal spams in my elbows. It felt like my veins filled with actual fire.

I didn't need to see Latoya's face to know she was lying. She really wanted to say, "This is going to hurt like hell. The pain gonna make you feel like a cartoon herniating through its eyes." It was only in May, three months ago, that man-related trauma sent me to the massage table. Could you blame me, Zev had left my heart squirming in pain. And it was May, and I was vulnerable, and I was in a strange country.

"Deep breaths, hold it." Latoya counts to three; she pinches my neck and turns my head to the left. Her new white walls are calming. I breathe. No fresh paint, the room doesn't smell. Only perfect lines. Try to find a spot of dirt, where the wallpapers meet.

"Holy. Holy Holy." The pain Latoya spoke about so nonchalantly struck me. "Stupid gym. Stupid hot guy. What the heck is a Devin?" I yelled.

"What have we learned?" Latoya placed a hot towel under my neck. She twists my head from side to side.

"Hot guys are the devil. Holy. Holy. Holy." Paying for a massage on Shabbat was justified as this was a medical emergency. The least I could do was not swear.

Latoya twisted my neck. "You don't need to listen to them. Never listen to them."

My week would have been more pleasant if I hadn't obeyed this random hot guy.

*

Latoya flipped me onto my belly and pressed her elbow deep into the muscles above my gluteus medius. Fig leaves flooded my periphery. "I haven't fully rid you of Rodrigo's trauma. Are you holding your stretches for a couple minutes?" Her fig tree was greener than it was the last time, more of those large, oddly shaped leaves as well. It was living for this record-breaking August weather.

I groaned, hoping she would take that as a yes. I tried not to lie on Shabbat. My mother would not approve.

"Rrrrrodrrrrrigo." My smile pressed into the soft cotton-covered face cushion. I moaned this time. Arched my back on instinct. "Rrrrrodrrrrrrigo." I stretched both *r*s. I couldn't relax my pelvis to the table. I forgot Rrrrrodrrrrrigo. I forgot most things about that May weekend in the desert; I figured that was the true sign of a weekend well spent in Nevada. Radical Faeries. The best. No one went to bed before 5 a.m. and each night a new man wanted to worship my tiny hole with their mouths, members, fingers, and toes. In the two months since Zev vanished into a cloud of dairy protein powder my heart remained shards blown away by a strong wind. It still wasn't spring in Newfoundland, so I took the chance to get an early start to wearing shorts in a foreign land. My heart was still on edge. I was susceptible and Rrrrrodrrrrrigo smelled like a cozy but wild campfire in the middle of a cedar grove.

"Yes, Rodrigo." Latoya spoke his name more quickly. Devoid of any romance or drama. Latoya remembers more about the men I have slept with than I do; she calls it her cross to bear.

It wasn't Rrrrrodrrrrrigo's fault why I was on the table this time in unbearable pain in the gross August heat. Rrrrrodrrrrrigo didn't do anything except be hot.

I spotted Rrrrrodrrrigo the moment I walked into the Monster Gym the Radical Faeries conference provided us attendees day passes to. He stood by the squat rack. His pink-and-blue tie-dyed crop top rolled over his round belly. I walked directly to the stacks of kettle bells beside him. Was he a fellow conference goer? Was he from the seminar on "The Ethical Use of Poppers Outside the Bedroom"? They passed out new samples of Rush, poppers that take the edge off for three seconds instead of the usual fifteen. Mind you, it is an intense three seconds that makes you think feel like you have been high for fifteen hours. I had too many samples. The organizers passed out flyers to warn that, while they do make anal sex spectacular, poppers are still technically a "highly caustic" "cleaning agent." I felt their air quotes.

"Can harm skin. Inhale responsibly." Ethics in action. Maybe he wasn't there. It wouldn't have been a good story to tell our future kids during Hanukkah anyways.

I prepared to squat. There was a loud whirring from the large grey tubes that hung a couple feet above my head. I spread my feet shoulder width apart. The grey walls above the mirrors didn't inspire a pump. I pulled my sweatpants down below my waist to show a bit of skin in case Rrrrrodrrrrrigo looked over. Thirty-two neck rotations and our eyes never met. His form was perfection. The way his butt rounded and extended behind his body. I would observe him until my visa expired, then suggest a green card marriage so I could keep watching his form forever.

Rrrrrodrrrrrigo adjusted his clear blue horn-rimmed glasses between sets. Was he in the session on consent in the kink community? "Butt Grommets and Harnesses Doesn't Mean You've Given the Green Light." There were poppers and mushrooms at that meeting as well as Faeries giving out lines in the third bathroom stall. He could have been there, I was, but I wasn't. Getting fucked up on the university's dime was epic. Getting fucked on the university's dime, fucking two thumbs-up. Meeting the love of my life on the university's dime, priceless. None of my friends, myself included, believed the Political Science department would cover my expenses for *this* conference, nor that the faculty strike didn't affect my funding.

"Excuse me." Rrrrrodrrrrrigo brushed by me to put another metal plate on the silver bar he was lifting. It was already laden with more than I could lift. He did not should me.

I did an impromptu head rotation. Inhaled quietly, yet, as if, it was my last breath on Earth. I dared my eyes to conceal the euphoria spreading inside my being. Rrrrrodrrrrrigo smelled like he could be the man to give me that white-picket-fence life. 2.5 kids and a two-car garage. His lips were just as full as mine and I wanted to feel them all over my body. I needed to show him my form. One of the twenty-five-pound kettle bells was already on the floor. Rrrrrodrrrrrigo lifted the bar off its rest stand onto his shoulders. If we did squats side by side, he couldn't help but fall in love with me. The other kettle bell was across from the water fountain. Rrrrrrodrrrrrigo squatted down deep. He rose slowly. His hips popped forward just slightly as he returned to the start position. He made me wish I walked around with gold stars. Rrrrrodrrrrigo did another squat. I weighed less than the combined number of weights he squatted. Being lifted was in my top three favourite pre-sex activities. I did a few neck rotations to ensure that Rrrrrodrrrrrigo was still squatting. He was. Zev smelled better, but I wasn't complaining. The TV in the corner played an ad for a foot spa. It would be nice to get home to St John's to one of those, if only I didn't have rent to pay. I wished I knew of a way to get the university to pay for the Deluxe Pedi Blaster 3000.

I stuck my ass out the appropriate amount.

One squat. Good.

Two, not bad.

I added a neck rotation to gauge if Rrrrrodrrrrrigo was impressed. Our children could have his bright hazel eyes. Not that anything was wrong with my brown ones. Three. Not great.

Rrrrrodrrrrigo put his bar to rest on the rack and stepped back to take in the work he had done on his quads. There were no notes I could have offered him. He flashed himself a quick smile and I knew he agreed. Rrrrrodrrrrrigo rubbed his hand through this high-top faded afro.

Four. Notice me. Five. Six. Seven. This is my personal best. Then I felt it. I hoped it was Rrrrrodrrrrigo's burning hand, but the warmth came from inside me. A vocalization of the collective frustrations of my joints and muscles being forced into performing seven weighted squats. Under the pressure of hot man. He was tall. He was so dark. He was beyond beautiful, cheekbones for days. A genuine tall, dark, and handsome hot guy. I felt like he was kind to his mom, just like I want our future kids to be.

"Deep breath." Latoya kneaded the knot in my lower back. "Ugh, Rodrigo. I don't think he was worth it."

He was worth it a little bit, I thought as I smiled into the face cushion. Latoya wasn't in the sauna when Rrrrrodrrrrigo said, "You should." The words gave me whiplash. Only two months since Zev first you shoulded me unsolicited. "You should keep your back straight when you squat. You could hurt yourself." He continued to *hombre escuela*. But was it mansplaining when he was right, and I already had hurt myself? Yes. I already knew what he was saying. I knew I had hot guy decent-smelling blinders on. He should have offered his unsolicited advice after my first repetition. I knew he had seen me.

"You're right, thanks, man." We entered the communal showers, ghost smells of Head & Shoulders 4 in 1 Sandalwood Anti-Dandruff Shampoo lingered. He offered me his camomile body wash. My sinuses had no reason to protest. Like a gentleman, Rrrrrodrrrrigo offered me a ride back to where I was staying. Latoya for sure wasn't there when Rrrrrodrrrrigo entered me in the back seat of his best friend's pine-scented blue Hyundai Accent hatchback. And again, in the alleyway outside the Faerie conference hotel.

"Faerie magic is the purest form. I'm Rrrrrodrrrrrigo." He drove over the steel bridge across the street from the hotel into the arid desert. No kids in our future after all. Regardless, I needed Latoya, but I was stuck in the sand dunes. Did that actually happen?

"One last deep breath." Latoya pushed deep into my tissues. The giant knot in my lower back released and my hips met the table again. "Rodrigo." Latoya rubbed both her hands over my back. A pleasant heat built up under her palms. "What have we learned from this?"

"Hot guys will be the death of me." I breathed deep. A rush of air flooded through the open window.

"Exactly. On your back, lovie. Let me try and grab hold of this neck again." Latoya removed the pillow under my hips. "Give me five deep breaths. I want you to breathe so deep that your expanding body moves my fingers." Latoya pinched my neck. "One."

I breathed. There was nothing but pain. It echoed through the middle of my left armpit. A large leaf had fallen off the fig tree. It had been over a hundred years since a fresh fig had grown in Newfoundland. I wished for another Zev.

"Did you at least get something out of it this time?"

"Not nearly enough."

*

On the day my current injury transpired, my gym reeked of Old Spice and crawled with retirees on the umpteenth hour of their workout. Doing the most to avoid their wives. A.K.A, a generic Tuesday afternoon at this wellness establishment. The hot guy who led me to the massage table for the summer edition of shoulding trauma was perched beside the lat machine when I arrived.

"It's free. I'm Devin." He curled thirty-five-pound dumbbells as he spoke. I hadn't seen him before. Was he a part of the influx of people who joined the gym since word got out the hot tub is bigger and jettier? I wished Zev were a part of the influx.

Devin looked like the kind of guy who insisted you immediately wipe off the molasses carton with a wet cloth to prevent an eternally sticky situation. Devin smelled like it too, lemon-scented geraniums. Comforting but antiseptic. He was so clean. Did he add a pre-emptive layer of dishwashing liquid on his hands before touching certain things? Quirky hot guys. I love.

No one had ever introduced themselves to me while actively lifting weights and I had been at this gym since before there was a hot tub. "I'm Prentis." I lied. This would have been a funny story we told our kids around the table during Passover when we threw the Haggadah out the window and dove into the brisket. "Forgive me, my real name is Martin." He smelled like store-bought white bread. I didn't get any hints of butter, which is good because of my irreconcilable differences with dairy. He could be the one.

Devin's eyes followed me in the mirror that spanned the length of the wall before us. Flecks of green dotted his eyes. A perfect round mole adorned the tip of his right ear. Devin had one dimple on the left side of his face. Everyone knows that one dimple is sexier than two. He wielded a polite closed-mouth smile. For sure a sign of meekness. From his stable jawbone and healthy facial structure, I knew he had beautiful, strong teeth that, when shown, ignite everything in their line of fire. Any more moves in the direction of Prince Charming would have sent me over the edge. His closed-mouth smile while polite, also told me he was disappointed by the way I carried out my exercises. Devin didn't smell as good as Zev, but who does? His bicep flexed into a naturally highlighted light-brown version of the rest of his skin. I hoped he was as into the hyperpigmentation of his body as I was. The pale spots on his face drove my eyes crazy. I wondered about the stretch marks on his ass. Art waiting to be revered. "You should lean back when you pull down." Devin's biceps were all I could focus on. I heard the "You should," but it was August and I was desperate for a summer fling. It had been five months since I last laid eyes on Zev, and three months since Rrrrrodrrrrrigo. But this hot guy was going to be different. I could hear my mother preaching of the pitfalls of lust in my ear.

The Sports TV played a live news segment. Members of the Wəlastəkwiyik Indigenous communities were given parcels of their land back from a large industry player, the AV Group, in the New Brunswick forestry industry. Chiefs of the Madawaska Maliseet and Sitansisk First Nations recognize this is the first step of its kind between the six nations and a large industry player. They were adamant the First Nations deserved a fair say in how their traditional lands are developed. This land back was ostensibly symbolic.

I leaned back symbolically. This was an exercise I knew inside out. Devin was someone I wouldn't have minded knowing inside out. All his muscles were bigger than mine.

"You should make sure your shoulders are back even more, right now they look like padlocked to your ears." Devin hurled the dumbbell in his hands towards the ceiling then towards the floor.

I obeyed. Did I mention he was a hot guy. I pulled the machine handles above my head towards my shoulders. The other TVs played basketball, world news, poker, and more basketball. The TV dedicated to sports analysis was off. Perseverance and the smell of sweat were enhanced by the stifling heat. The air conditioner vent poured cool air over me. One last set to go. The TV playing the weather program announced the heat wave would last another three days. "Record-breaking temperatures for August in St John's, Newfoundland, 35.2 degrees. A spot previously held by the August 14, 1876, 33.9 degrees."

The lat pull-down machine meant romance. A meet cute by the squat rack was trouble. We could tell our future kids about this proudly on the way to shul. I leaned back and pulled the one hundred pounds I was lifting before with all my strength. On the arduous journey back to the start position, an eruption of cold and hot chills paraded through my shoulders. The one hundred pounds of weight plates I attempted to lift slammed onto the pile of iron below. My subscapularis had had enough. It rebelled in the only way it knew I would take seriously.

One by one, I released my fingers and let my hands fall from the overhead machine handles into my lap.

Devin nodded and leaned into a set of standing chest fly exercises with the same 35 lbs weights. Wild.

I reached for my phone to ask Latoya if she could see me right away. I breathed deep, but only because I thought I was dying. The desire to keep smelling fizzled. He didn't even smell that good.

"I don't know what you have got done to this neck, my duckie. It is just not pretty at all. Always reduce the weight when you attempt any exercise in a new position. How many times do I need to tell you, your body needs time to adjust? These damn men." Latoya poured sweet almond oil in her palms and returned to my stressed subscapularis. I writhed more as the knots gave way to the pressure of Latoya's precisely placed pointers. Her thumb pressed deep into my neck, trying to cleanse me from my susceptibility to the should-isms and the men who love to go around unsolicitedly shoulding at unsuspecting strangers.

My eyes scanned her studio for anything to distract her from my poor taste in men. A new stem had shot up out of the top of the fig tree. Below it was a large, round green fruit.

"A fig? For real?" It hurt my neck to look at it, but I needed to see it in this moment.

"All it needed was TLC. They are so juicy, and sweet. Hard work growing a Mediterranean fruit in the middle of the North Atlantic Ocean." Latoya went on about the perils of indoor gardening and the time it took to finesse the lighting schedule. "I'll give you a cutting before you leave."

If a fresh fig could grow in Newfoundland, then anything was possible. Baruck HaShem. Maybe a hot guy will not be the death of me.

Corinna Chong

LOVE CREAM HEAT

When Louisa pulled up to the house, her mother was standing on the driveway. She was holding a green cooler and an electric carving knife in one hand and an antelope head by the horn in the other.

"Mom," Louisa said as she opened her door, "you look crazy."

"Hi sweetheart," she said, setting down the cooler and balancing the knife and the head on its lid. "Give us a squish."

Her face wasn't red or puffy from crying, but as they came together for a hug Louisa could not help but notice that her mother's fingers, under the nails, were blue.

"How you doin', Mom?" Louisa said into her mother's woolly shoulder, which emanated some vanilla-choked perfume that she'd never smelled on her before.

"I was just cleaning some things out of the garage," she said. "No sense waiting for you and Cole when there's just so *much*."

"Cole's not here yet?"

"Sunday morning," she said. The day of the funeral.

"Bastard," Louisa muttered.

"I know. You probably heard *she* isn't coming." Cole had moved to Singapore with his wife eight years ago, suddenly ordaining Louisa as the recipient of daily phone calls from their mother about suspicious moles, suspicious neighbours, computers that hate her, and the latest garage sale finds. Their mother's resentment over being robbed of her favourite child expressed itself in her refusal to call Mei-Ling by her name.

"I'm happy you're here. It's a little unnerving being by myself in this big house." She passed the cooler and the knife to Louisa and hooked her arm around the neck of the antelope. "Now help me get this stuff to Goodwill, please." She gestured to a half-empty box sitting at the curb.

"Mom. Poor people don't want Dad's dead animal heads."

"Well I don't know. I can't exactly throw them away. They remind me too much of him." She turned the antelope's face toward herself and studied it at arm's length. "It's the eyes, I think. So pensive."

Louisa knew that grief came in waves, but it bothered her that her mother seemed so resigned to her father's death already, as though he'd been long gone for years. They busied themselves with sorting through his things well into the evening, and by the end of the day her mother had yet to shed a single tear. Once Louisa had retreated to her room for the night, she took out her phone and googled "stages of grief." Most of what she found confirmed things she already knew. Denial, anger, bargaining, depression, acceptance. But was there such a thing as progressing too quickly? Louisa doubted it was truly acceptance if you skipped some of the stages to get there.

Her mind began to wander back to Michener. She'd spent the entire drive to Saskatoon like this, drifting in and out of memories of their time together. What she'd loved most about Michener was his rice cooker. It was the most intimate part of their relationship. Two cups of rice, three and a quarter cups of water, seventeen minutes. It was the only thing they could cook, so sometimes, after sex, they'd sit on the carpet in his dorm room and eat it by the bowlful, topped with chunks of butter and soy sauce drizzled from little plastic packets. The steam from the cooker hung in clouds around them. What would they talk about? She couldn't remember now. But it hadn't mattered. Common interests were of little concern back then. It was all about fucking, even though fucking was five minutes of missionary on a single bed, she practising her breathiest moan with each clumsy thrust. Michener always pulled out at the last moment despite her being on the pill.

"Sorry," he'd say, finishing himself off while she wiped up with a sock.

Now, after almost twenty years, Louisa found herself longing for Michener. She'd barely given him a thought after they'd parted ways. She knew he'd married the woman he began dating right after her. Rebound Rayleen, Louisa and her friends called her. Rayleen was pale and wafer-thin and considerably taller than Michener, so they made a comically mismatched pair. They'd only been twenty-one. There was a good chance they were divorced by now. He'd stopped posting on Facebook years ago, which suggested he didn't have much to be proud of.

She closed her browser and clicked on the Facebook Messenger app.

Hi Michener, it's been a while! I hope you're well. I'm in town and wondered if you might be interested in catching up? I know a good place for rice. ;)

She stared at the words for a while, reading and rereading and imagining what Michener would think when he saw it. Was it too provocative? Or not enough? She thought of that sly little smile of his, the one that always came on his face when they were taking off their clothes. In the end she deleted the winky face and hit Send.

*

Cole wrestled with his tie and jacket in the car on the way to the funeral home. His plane had been delayed, so he'd swept in only just in time for the service.

"Must be nice." Louisa drove, eyes on the road.

"Yeah, this is nice," he replied, smoothing his hair in the mirror. "Do you know what a nervous wreck I've been? I've had zero time to process anything."

"Me neither. Our mother is in full purge mode. It's weird. It's like she feels liberated or something."

"It was a long time coming, I guess." Cole sniffed. It took Louisa a few moments to realize that tears were dripping silently from his cheeks and landing on his shirt.

"Cole," she said. "It's okay. You'll wreck your shirt."

"It's not fucking okay," he said.

After the funeral, Cole wolfed down three egg salad sandwiches, a pile of browning fruit, two oatmeal raisin cookies, and a slice of lemon meringue pie. Louisa couldn't eat. She dabbed at her swollen eyes with fraying tissues.

"So many sandwiches," their mother remarked as the guests filtered out. "We'll be eating sandwiches until next week!" She clapped her hands.

Cole sat in a chair in the corner of the hall, his legs stuck out in a V in front of him.

"You okay?" Louisa asked, tapping the sole of his shoe with hers.

He said nothing at first, staring off into the distance. Then: "Is she—*blue?*" he asked. He was looking at their mother as she hugged the last of the guests.

"You noticed too? Her hands?"

"Yeah. Her hands, but also all over too. Look at her face, for Christ sakes."

It was true; Louisa hadn't noticed until now. It was probably the black dress she wore, or maybe the fluorescent lighting, that was bringing out the blue tinge of her skin.

"You ask her," Cole said. "I'm just—exhausted."

Louisa rolled her eyes. "Because you're the only one."

"You don't understand," he said, rubbing his face in his palms. He looked up at Louisa with bloodshot eyes. "Mei-Ling is pregnant," he said.

"Oh," she said, pulling up a chair next to him. "Wow. That's—great!"

"No. No Louisa, it's not great." He rubbed his face again.

"Okay. Sorry."

"We agreed not to have kids. Neither of us ever wanted them."

"Yeah, I know. So was it an accident?"

"I don't know. She says it was. But then I found six unopened packs of birth control pills in her bedside table."

"Jeez," she said. "But wait—how do you know? I mean, it doesn't necessarily mean she deliberately stopped taking them. They could just be … extra."

"I know. But I just have a feeling. Plus, she refuses to get an abortion."

"What? Why?"

"I don't know! She said something like now that the thing is in there, she just can't bear to get rid of it."

"What a bitch."

Cole glared at her. "Not helping."

"Well what're you gonna do?"

"I dunno." He sighed. "Maybe … maybe move back here for a bit."

"Cole. Come on. You're not thinking about abandoning your pregnant wife, are you?"

"Fuck. Just because she's pregnant now she can be completely manipulative and I just have to go along with it?"

"She's your wife, Cole. You made a vow."

"Since when do you take that stuff seriously?"

"I don't. I just mean that this isn't just some girl you knocked up. You're not eighteen anymore."

"I didn't sign up for this!" he said, standing and raising his hands in the air. "Plus my dad just fucking *died*. And I was way the hell in another country."

Their mother turned to him then, raising a hand to her mouth. The lingering guests made a quick exit, eyes downcast. Cole stormed out after them.

*

It was three days before she received a reply from Michener.

Hey Lou, long time no see! I've been thinking about you, actually. Would love to hang out.

Louisa felt a rush of heat in her groin as she read the message. She imagined kissing Michener wetly, pressing him up against a wall.

Tomorrow night? she wrote back.

They arranged to meet at the Silver Dragon downtown. As soon as she was shown to a vinyl booth in a dingy corner of the restaurant, she felt overdressed in her leopard print dress with a scooped neckline. Michener had not yet arrived. She ordered a bottle of Tsingtao and waited, picking at the label. She tightened the straps of her dress to cover a bit of her cleavage.

He showed up seven minutes late, wearing jeans and a Rough-riders jersey. He smiled and waved as he came towards her.

Fat, was the first thought that came to her. She immediately felt ashamed. Her mind raced with regret over her outfit; why hadn't she just dressed in jeans like she usually did?

"Green machine!" she said, letting him give her a tentative, sweaty hug with one arm.

"Yeah," he chuckled. "How are you? You look great." He kept looking down at the table. When he sat, he plucked at the sleeves of his jersey to untuck the fabric from his armpits.

"Aw, thanks," she said. "You too."

This had been a bad idea. A terrible idea. Any desire she'd had for Michener had completely dissolved the moment she saw him. He looked like a dad—like the dad of someone they had been friends with back when they were going out. Evidently he was uncomfortable too; he'd picked up the laminated menu and was examining it, flipping the pages.

"I haven't been here in a while," he said. "Is it still the same?"

"I'm not super hungry," Louisa said. "We don't have to eat."

"Oh," he said, setting down the menu. "But, maybe we should at least get something small? They have fries here, I think."

Fries. Fries at a Chinese restaurant. Her Chinese relatives on her father's side would have balked. Louisa felt pathetic, sitting there with him.

"Um, sure," she said.

He ordered, and added a Coke for himself.

"I'm glad you messaged me," he said when the server had left. Louisa smiled. Her gut sank. Was he still expecting to have sex? What would she do?

"How's your wife?" she asked. "Rayleen, right?"

"Yeah, good memory. She's good." Not divorced, clearly. Louisa saw now that he wore a gold wedding band. "She's in Toronto on business," he said. "She's away a lot." His finger traced the water ring left on the table from his Coke glass. "And yours?" he continued. "Sorry, I can't remember his name…"

"Nate," she said. "I'm not sure, actually. Divorced. Three years ago now." She held up her ringless hand.

"Oh man," he said, "I'm sorry." She could see in the glint of his eyes that it was a small triumph for him.

"Don't be," she said. "I'm not! It's pretty great being free."

His lips pressed together, then rolled back out with a tiny pop. "I hope I didn't …" he began, "uh … contribute to that. In any way."

"Huh?" she said. "What do you mean?"

She understood now. He did want to have sex. In his mind, she had been pining for him all of these years. He was the one that got away.

"Another one, please," she called out to the server, lifting her empty bottle. She had a desperate urge to get roaring drunk. "You wanna do a shot?" she asked him.

Michener laughed. "Naw, I'm good." When they had dated, Michener's drink of choice at parties was a mickey of Captain Morgan rum, which he would polish off handily by the end of the night.

"Okay," he said. "Here goes. I've kind of … wanted to say something to you for a long time."

Shit, thought Louisa. This was going to be painful. He was going to ask her for sex, just ask her outright, like a sad little puppy dog. She had not come prepared for this. What would she say? Refusing him, seeing the disappointed look on his chubby face, would be too awful to bear.

She would agree. Yes. She would just do it anyway. How bad could it really be? He would be grateful, after all, and that was a bit of a turn-on.

"All right," she said. "But can I just ask you something first?"

"Sure." He picked up his Coke and took a sip.

"Does your wife know you're here with me?" she said.

"Yeah. Why?"

"Oh, okay. I just wanted to know if, you know. She was okay with it."

"She's not the jealous type," he said.

"That's good."

The server arrived with the fries and another beer. Louisa ordered a shot of tequila and shoved a fry in her mouth. It burned her tongue.

"Hot," she said, spitting it out. She rolled it up into her napkin. Michener watched her, smoothing his eyebrow. She remembered now that it was a nervous habit of his.

"Anyway," he said. "Uh … okay. This is awkward."

Louisa took a long swig of beer. She held the bubbling liquid in her mouth, letting it cool her tongue, before gulping it down. She imagined how things would start. Michener would kiss her, very softly at first. His lips looked dry and flaky. His hands would press into the small of her back and he'd grip the underside of her bare thigh, pulling it up on his hip.

"So I wanted to apologize," he said.

Louisa went blank. She held his gaze, stunned. She could feel her face flushing.

"For things I may have done," he added. "Back when we were dating, you know? It was a long time ago, but … I've just felt bad about it. For a while now."

"I …" Louisa said. "I guess I'm not sure what you mean. Apologize for what, exactly?"

Michener's eyes shot up to the ceiling as he scrubbed his hair. "Oh man, okay. This is hard. I guess I've realized in the last few years that I was a dick back then. So I wanted to apologize for … for forcing you. For forcing you to have sex with me. I know it happened a lot."

"Oh," Louisa said. Her head spun. Was it the beer? As if on cue, her shot arrived. She didn't want it anymore; she remembered now that she'd hated the taste of tequila ever since she puked it up at a party in university. Michener had probably been there.

"You don't have to forgive me though," he said. "I mean, I know it's pretty unforgivable."

"No, it's okay," she said. She felt angry now, all of a sudden. How the tables had turned—he now the assured and righteous one, and she the damaged, pitiable one. She took three fries and munched them. He sipped his Coke, watching her.

Her mind was reeling through the memories of all the times they'd slept together. She could only seem to recall bits and pieces. She had no recollection of any arguments they had over sex. She had no recollection of feeling like she hadn't wanted to have sex. Somewhere deep down, though, she thought she remembered a feeling of repulsion—a lump, dense but pliable, like a gristly, chewed-up wad of beef, that she carried around in her throat all the time but forced herself to ignore. Her impulse now was to yell at Michener, tell him to fuck off with his apology.

"What inspired all this anyway?" she said instead. "Did you spend your youth fucking hordes of girls or something?"

He flinched at the word *fucking*. His eyes went to his Coke, which he swirled in the glass.

"Well no," he said. "After you I married Rayleen. That was it."

She wanted to throw something at him. She could toss the shot in his face. "I think I need to go," she said.

*

She cried in the cab on the way home, swigging tequila straight from a bottle she'd picked up at a corner liquor store outside the restaurant. In the months before their separation, Nate had kept calling her "frigid" because she wouldn't have sex with him. At the time she'd thought it was because she'd fallen out of love with him. Now, however, she questioned whether it was something else, some past trauma she'd forgotten about, or perhaps blocked out. Had Michener really forced her? She thought about how she felt raw sometimes, how it would hurt to sit down…

And then she was back at the funeral, sitting in the front row between Cole and her mother during the ceremony. An elaborate, stinking arrangement of lilies spilled over the casket. Louisa had always hated lilies—their sour smell, a festering. Even so, she had been grateful the casket was closed. She hadn't wanted to see her father's face, hollowed by chemo, his eyelids like brittle shells, waxed shut. In the eulogy, Louisa's aunt, his sister, had described his final days, how he'd greeted her with a smile each morning. How even at the very end, he did not struggle. He let go, peacefully, without complaint, without protest.

Heads had bobbed across the room, nodding in affirmation of her father's bravery. At the time Louisa had been numb, nodding along, but thinking back on it now, she wanted to scream. She couldn't help but picture her father, his body flattened against the hospital bed like an empty sac, a smiling fool, as if he was enjoying himself. As if he wanted the pain, craved the burn of toxic chemicals pulsing through his veins. This wasn't bravery, Louisa knew. It was submission. Pure weakness.

When she got back to the house, Cole and her mother were watching TV in the dark.

"How was your friend?" Cole asked, not looking up.

"Fine," Louisa replied. "Hasn't changed a bit."

In the glow of the TV, her mother's skin seemed ultraviolet.

Louisa grabbed the remote and pressed the power button. The screen went black.

"Hey, what gives?" Cole said.

Louisa flicked on the lights. "We need to do something about your skin, Mom. You need to get yourself checked out."

Their mother scoffed. "Excuse me? What, pray tell, is the matter with my skin?" She looked incredulously at Cole, then at Louisa.

"Do we need to do this now?" Cole said. "You haven't even taken off your coat."

"Your skin is *blue,* Mom. Look at your fingers."

She did, then laughed a little. "Oh that," she said. "You had me thinking something was really the matter."

"It's not okay," Louisa said. "Blue skin is not normal, Mom."

"Oh please, Louisa. Don't be so dramatic. It's just the colloidal silver," she said.

"The what?" Cole said.

"It's a treatment I've been taking. A mineral supplement."

"Taking how?" Louisa asked. "Like you've been drinking silver?"

"Well, not *drinking*. Just small doses, two tablespoons a day. And the cream as well."

"You've been rubbing silver cream all over yourself?" Cole said.

"My goodness, you two! It's perfectly safe. Gwyneth Paltrow uses it. They said that a slight bluing of the skin is normal."

"Gwyneth Paltrow is a kook, Mom. I thought everyone knew that." Louisa tore off her coat and pitched it on the chair.

"I know it's controversial," she said. "But I believe it. It makes me feel better."

"This is insane," Louisa said. "You're poisoning yourself, you know that? I have to go to bed. I drank too much."

"Speaking of poison," her mother said, sinking back into the couch and turning the TV back on.

"And another thing," Louisa yelled over the audio. "Why aren't you upset at all about Dad? It's like you don't even care."

Her mother gaped at Cole. He shrugged.

"Oh, come on. Don't pretend like it doesn't bother you too, Cole."

"*Lou*-isa Jean." Her mother slapped her thigh with the palm of her hand. "Listen. I'm sorry I'm not a puddle of self-pity, since that's what you seem to want me to be. What can I say? I've made my peace with it. There's no changing it. No sense dwelling on it." She crossed her arms. "No one ever got anywhere by dwelling. You should go to bed."

*

The next morning, Louisa woke with a pounding headache. She could hear her mother putting dishes away in the kitchen downstairs. She crept into her mother's ensuite bathroom and got a couple of ibuprofens from the medicine cabinet. There on the shelf was a brown glass bottle with a screw-top. The label said *Silver Supreme* in yellow scripted letters against a cartoony illustration of a crescent moon and stars. She unscrewed it and sniffed. It smelled like nothing. She tipped the contents down the drain and set the empty bottle back on the shelf.

When she got to the bottom of the stairs, she saw Cole's suitcase by the door. She stalked into the kitchen and found him sitting at the table with a mug of coffee. Her mother was scrambling eggs at the stove.

"Why are you all packed?" she asked.

"Morning," said Cole. "My plane leaves today. Remember?"

"What the hell? You're going back?"

Cole blew on his coffee. "Um, yeah. I do live there after all."

"What about all that stuff you said?"

Cole sighed. "I was upset, Louisa. I'd just buried my dad."

"My dad too," she shot back.

"Yeah, *our* dad. People are sometimes irrational when bad things happen, you know."

"Clearly. I feel like I'm the only one around here who's not completely irrational."

"Honey," her mother said, holding up a spatula. "I know this is hard for you. But you're being nasty. Just leave your brother alone. He's got a lot to deal with right now."

"Fine," she said. "Have fun dealing with the baby you don't even want."

That was the last thing she said to her brother before he went back to Singapore, back to his normal life. She'd sobbed in her room for two hours and then regretted not giving him a proper goodbye. But eventually, when she'd packed up her own things and driven back to Winnipeg, gotten settled back into her apartment and back to work, her memory of that week began to fuzz over like everything else, the sting dissipating with each passing day. Instead, other memories began to surface for her. Older memories. Memories of her dad.

Once, back when she was in junior high, she'd asked her dad how she would know what being in love felt like. She'd started dating her first boyfriend then, and what she'd really wanted was some kind of veiled permission to give up her virginity. She worried, however, that he might be embarrassed by the question. But instead, he smiled warmly, and thanked her for asking him instead of her mother. He told her that love would feel like losing control. It would feel like she would do anything, absolutely anything for the guy.

"To be honest," he'd said, "it might feel a bit scary at first. You're a strong girl. You like being in control. But with love, you have to just let go."

It had been one of her most heartwarming memories of her father. They'd never been all that close, but in that moment, she'd felt so loved, so connected to him. Now she felt differently about it. She realized now that in his naive fatherly way, he hadn't even considered the possibility that she might want to have sex at fourteen years old. That she would have sex, and that afterwards she would feel new on the outside—like the world had shifted into some alternate dimension where the colours were bold and lurid—and yet old on the inside. Carved out and emptied. Surely her father would have said something different if he'd known.

At the end of July, Louisa received a text message from her brother at 2:23 a.m. She'd fallen asleep with her phone wedged beneath her, and the buzz against her ribs startled her onto her hands and knees like a spooked cat. It was the middle of a freak heat wave, and even though she'd shed all of her clothes she was sweating, her hair sticky on her forehead.

There was no text in the message; just a photo of a tiny red baby on a weigh scale, screaming. The face was ghastly—bloated, frozen in a tortuous grimace. Its fists were held up by its ears as if railing against its cruel new surroundings. Was it a boy or a girl? Louisa couldn't tell.

Another photo pinged onto her screen. In this one, Mei-Ling was wearing a hospital gown and cradling the baby to her chest, and Cole was snuggled up against her with his hand on the baby's downy black head. They were smiling, Cole more than Mei-Ling.

Congratulations! she typed back. *So precious.* She quickly deleted the last sentence. There was nothing precious about the baby or the parents. Cole's face, in fact, was as repellent to her as the baby's with its plastered grin, the edges of his teeth peeking out from his top lip with an eerie shine on them, as if they were made of plastic. *Your hearts must be bursting,* she typed instead. But before she could hit Send, her phone shut off. She tapped the screen. Nothing. She fiddled with the power switch. A notification came up:

Temperature. iPhone needs to cool down before you can use it.

Was it really that hot in her room? She was suddenly aware that her sheets were soaking wet. How had she not noticed?

She went to the thermostat. Thirty-two degrees. The A/C had crapped out. She flung open the sliding door to her balcony, and outside it was considerably cooler. Her apartment had been cooking, stewing in the muggy air trapped from the heat of the day. She stood on the balcony, naked, letting the night air chill her clammy skin. She could see a few stars between the dark clouds winking over the city lights speckled below. The acrid smell of a deep fryer rose up from an unseen food truck. Someone yelled in the street, drunk or crazy or maybe both, his echoing words indecipherable. Louisa closed her eyes, overwhelmed by her senses in her half-awake state.

Another forgotten memory now crawled its way out of the cracks of her mind. She and Michener, licking out their butter-slicked bowls, their tongues chasing the last grains of rice.

"Shit," Michener had said when he opened the cupboard to put away the bag of rice. Louisa looked inside. A scattering of brown pellets. Shit. Rat shit. The pellets were nearly identical in size and shape to the rice they'd just licked up. Her stomach turned, the congealed mass of rice inside flipping like a dreaming body.

She hadn't forgotten. Not really. She'd simply put it all away, tucked it inside where it couldn't be seen. That way, she could hold on to everything as if it were buried treasure.

All the way over in Singapore, the next day was already more than halfway over. Cole was a father now. His world had been altered, for better or for worse. For some reason, Louisa thought of the antelope head that her mother had eventually thrown away. She saw it now with its blank, glossy eyes, although it was no longer just a head. It was attached to a tiny human body, fists waving in the air.

There's just so much, her mother had said.

Beth Downey

THE BEE GARDEN

It was after they lost it that Ivan decided about the garden. Spring was well in now. The worst of it was over. He had work enough to make ends meet but they were menial jobs, for anyone with experience, and time weighed waxy on his hands.

He'd thought first of an elaborate rose bed. Muted colours like a sunset: purples and tangerine shades layered in together with the usual pink. Perhaps with some other things in for accents. Delphs maybe. He wanted something to give her that wouldn't insult their loss. Something to comfort her, honour her. But not to cheer her up. He said none of this, of course, and when the girl at the greenhouse asked in her crisp green apron whether they were trying to attract bees to the yard—"these are best kind: all the baby colours, *Monarda*, some lovely bells"—he decided that was a better story. So that's how he told it to Abigail.

She'd cried when she saw it started. On a grey Friday afternoon she came out the kitchen door to find black, loamy beds where patchy sod had been before. She'd kissed him. A real kiss, more vocal than any word or touch they had shared in recent weeks. Still Ivan felt somehow bashful, and the drive to dig deeper than his helplessness returned. "I want to hear this place really humming in summer," he said, turning back to the bow rake, "see them going in and out, you know?"

*

Weeks crumbled between his blackened palms as the backyard conformed itself to his vision. He taped newspaper over the glass in the back door and kitchen window to hide his progress. He filled evenings, weekends, any crevice of spare time with the work, folding into bed at night sore and spent. She climbed in after him, always working late—sometimes so he didn't remember.

Often, he woke to her hand drifting over his feet as she traced the edge of the bed through the dark. A draft, a jostle, a tender stab of cold. He groaned and untensed himself, gently pulling her closer behind him.

"Sorry," she whispered.

"I don't think that means what you think it means," he said, trapping her icy feet between his calves. "Sadistic fiend."

Her smile and breath spread over his shoulder. "I know. You're just so much warmer than I am."

"This is true. I have this thing they call a blood supply."

They were quiet. When she spoke again, the hum in her voice was gone, replaced by a rattle.

"You're far too good to me."

"No such thing," he said, craning over to kiss her. But he found the deadness there too.

All that summer, any time she wasn't locked in the office, or teaching, or travelling, or long in the bath, or long in their bed,

Ivan let Abbie help assemble trellises and staking. She seemed happy enough to participate, and it was a way to bring her close. Besides, the demand was endless. Windproofing, he figured, was something they understood. So they talked about work or things they'd read and sometimes about the future, but mostly he made her laugh as much as possible. He was good at it, on the right day, and they both missed the exercise. "God, I dies at you. Who thinks of that?" she said one afternoon, wiping her eyes.

"Don't die," he smiled.

"Okay."

The first time either of them heard her say something like that to anyone but family, they had been dating almost a year, and she impulsively professing love. These days, in the new world order of listening at doors, of euphemism and selective silence, it brought a welcome certainty. It was one of her tells. Abbie was home.

Still, the majority of the time Ivan's wife was off the edge of the map to him. A known-unknown that gently rasped against his mind like the buzz congregating in his soup tins. They seemed unlikely little devices, these "bee hotels" the greenhouse girl had put him on to—just tin cans jammed full of bamboo shoots for comb. But out of the three he'd set up, each one fixed to the top of an obelisk where it wouldn't shake, two were already in use. Hopeful, he set up two more of his own: reclaimed facing bricks, the kind with little holes in them, attached to the fence or a tree at the proper height.

*

Weeks droned out months as Ivan lost himself in the sciences of Eden. Blooming times, pest control, a balance of annuals and perennials, which plants needed how much structural support, how soil pH could impact a flower's hue. By the time everything was finished, Ivan had just about figured the logistics well enough to hope that, next year, it would be perfect. Even now, he had to admit it was close:

Hostas, plum and opalescent hydrangeas good enough for Monet; lavenders, lupins, bee balm, blue poppies; low, listening violets and creeping thyme, gentians in three varieties (*not every man has gentians in his house, in Soft September at slow, sad Michaelmas*); drooping foxgloves; wild, heart-bare anemones— the frank, familiar Canadians in white, but an Asian variety too, with pearl-pink petals each like the inside of a cockle shell; delphiniums, giant columbine, and every variety of rose that ever withstood the climate. She had them all. There was even a little bonsai in a rock garden, for peace, but that was an indulgence, a him-thing. And everywhere there winked a shadowy glitter of bees.

The gentians were as much as he'd ventured by way of allusion, always dangerous with Abbie's type. He had learned early on, if there was a metaphor, a reference, a subtext he could find in something, she had already thought of three. It made him careful. Too careful, could be. He knew she lay awake at night thinking things, wishing he did too, and he resented himself for being such a ready sleeper. Not that he didn't think things. Not that he wasn't pacing the cage inside himself just like her. But she had friends she talked to about the heady stuff. Old friends, good people. And silence was better, he told himself, in this case, than saying the wrong thing. So he hauled topsoil and shoveled mulch and he cut the edging in deep, and he did not say the wrong thing. Not in passing, not in bed, and not here. No bachelor's buttons, no monkshood. He'd thought of bleeding hearts for a minute, the white ones, but decided against them. Too close.

Where pain was planted in that garden, Ivan had planted it deep: it was in the soil, in the colours running through filamental plant veins. It was even in the vertiginous perfumes wafting secretly from the very tiniest blooms: grape hyacinth or sweet alyssum. This, Ivan thought, was breath for breath and pulse for pulse. Their hope, their grief, their need, brought into the world as work, as a becoming. Not a script. Not something you said.

And she didn't say anything, when he brought her out blindfolded to where the sunlight touched her feet. She just held him, tight.

"Do you like it?"

She nodded against his chest. "Thank you."

*

Abbie drank so many cups of tea in that garden, as summer cooled and autumn came and the colours refused to quit, grading papers on a kitchen chair all muffled up in one of his sweaters, that he paused one day taking down the bee hotels, now empty. *Arbour swing,* he thought. And it was so.

Christmas night Ivan angled the man-sized box out of his in-laws' back porch and stood it up beside the tree, delighted with himself. Abigail's father was the grand dojo master of surprises, so the stakes were high. Ivan tiptoed down the hall and through the chaste spare-bedroom murk to lay beside her, a hot water bottle cooling at her feet. Between the sounds of her breath and the ticking of unfamiliar clocks, he dropped off with a teen-aged suitor's sweaty palms.

The next day, surrounded by a dozen pairs of eager eyes and

decadent carnage of french toast, she received the box with a kind of gleeful trepidation. Embarrassed, she passed him a slender necklace box in return. He made a show of shaking it, pulling faces, then set it in his lap to watch her tear away. She gasped and beamed, chirping and turning the giant box over and over. "What's the weight limit on this thing?" she asked no one in particular, peering at the fine print.

"I'm not sure," he said, peeling tape off the ends of his parcel. "It sits two, though."

"I allow it does," he heard her say, just in time to register that he was looking at a positive pregnancy test. Ivan looked up, and crumbled.

*

No depth of snow could hamper their joy that winter. Though naturally, the Avalon did its best. Along the sidewalks in town a timeline of grit and sagging off-white layers cut visible now and then by the plow slowly compressed, dissolved, hardened into ice documenting winter's cruel caprice: January, February, March. But at home, off the main road and up the hill, the weight of time was finally beginning to lift for Ivan and Abbie. Every moment was a contest between the thrill of anticipation and the joy of savouring, wishing it all to go on forever. On April 1, Abigail found her swing standing naked in the snowy bee garden, at the end of a trail of size-eleven holes two feet deep in drift.

"What did you do!" she gasped, gaping out the kitchen window over her suspended cup.

"I couldn't help myself," he said, enfolding her from behind, breathing them in. "I want it to be ready first thing, as soon as the snow melts." She was barely showing, but he liked to lay his hand over all that was happening underneath.

"My dear, you got to be cracked tramping through all that for me," she said.

"Yes maid, some foolish," he said, in the hammy imitation that made her cringe-laugh. "But you knows, my duck: I'm nobody's fool except yours."

*

Miraculously, warmth followed soon after and stayed. Three weeks on, the bee hotels were up again with first visitors scoping out digs, and first green pushing through the frost. Abigail, exhausted and buried in end-of-term paperwork, was crawling out of her skin for a chance to enjoy it. "I am too big and too stiff to be cooped up indoors *anymore*," she said, getting into bed with some effort.

"Do you know what you are?" he asked her, propping his head on one elbow.

She opened one eye. "Are you about to be funny?"

"You," he said, brushing hair from her face, "are a bumblebee. You make no aerodynamic sense. But you work anyway."

". . . I think I can roll with that," she said.

"You might have to."

Five frigid toes paid him back for it. The pair settled. Ivan snuffed out the light. Everything was dark, but the dark was still awake.

"Nature violates nature," she said softly. "Just means we don't understand things, doesn't it."

"Hm?"

"I think you're more the bee than I am. I figure nature's pretty much got me roped."

He thought on that but didn't say anything. He felt as though she'd skipped something.

"You're impossible," she said. "I've always known that. Impossibly real, impossibly mine. I don't always know what to do with that."

"Hm. That makes two of us." He kissed her on the forehead. "Sweet dreams, Abbie." He ducked his head under the covers and nuzzled into the mound of her belly: "Sweet dreams, Cabbage." Then he rolled over and went to sleep. He was nearly gone when she spoke again.

"It's the wingbeat, you know. They figured it out."

"What?"

"She turns her wings over on the upstroke, so she gets lift both ways."

"That right."

"That's how she stays up."

"Mm."

*

The next morning, his day off, rude vibrations on the far side of the bed startled Ivan from his sleep. He flopped over, bleary-eyed, and found Abigail's phone reminding her to take her vitamin. He punched in her pass code to silence the thing, and a text thread showed open where the alarm had disappeared. It was between Abbie and an old friend in Montreal.

> *What's your blood type?—*
> *—O positive.*
> *Thanks—*

Ivan blinked at the phone. He scrolled up. The last exchange was months old: a picture of a positive pregnancy test and two words from Abbie. *Thank you.* The reply was equally brief: *When can I call?*

Ivan rolled back over and stared at the ceiling, making mental origami of the words. He lay there for a long time. When he got up he felt automated, like his mind was hanging, floating through space while his body went about the plan it had devised for the situation. He dressed, he drank a glass of water, he turned the heat down in the bedroom and the office, he took his coat and keys and climbed into the car, and then he was at the top of Signal Hill. He must have stopped for coffee on the way, since he had coffee. It sat there in his hand, steaming. The hill was quiet at that hour, mostly windblown joggers keeping to themselves. Ivan got out of the car and wandered along the low stone wall. He sat down with his coffee, the harbour narrows on his right. He sat there a long time.

*

That afternoon, Abigail called out to her husband. She dumped her keys and bag and wandered through the kitchen to the bedroom, grabbing an apple on her way. She knocked on the bedroom door, listening. "Ivan?" No answer. She opened the door and dropped her apple, unseating in the process a bee. The bee hovered near her face a moment before whining away to baffle itself against the window. The apple lodged where it had rolled, half under her desk in the corner of the room. The desk from her office. Ivan had pushed the bed over to make space for it. And his nightstand was gone.

She threw open the closet: decimated. She went to the office:

bookshelf still there, crib there, futon there, Ivan's nightstand beside it. His clothes were in hampers on the floor. Heart pounding, she moved to check her phone, but it wasn't on her. She padded back to the kitchen for a glass, a faint hum of panic pricking her ears. She found the bee and trapped it in the glass, delivering it out the kitchen door into the yard. As it floated back to the garden, its pitch-skewed hum doubled the one in her brain. Again, Abbie turned inward. She recovered her phone and checked for messages from Ivan, wandering back to the kitchen as she looked. Nothing there. She slipped it back in her pocket, checked the fruit bowl and the plants on the windowsills for any other rogue bees. Then, out of the corner of her eye, she noticed the oven light on. She reached out and felt the glass door, cool to her touch, then bent to peer through the spattered little window. Inside on the rack sat a brick with small holes in it, a scrap of paper pinned underneath. She opened the door and pulled out the note.

For your cold feet.

Allison Graves

CEILING LIKE THE SKY

One hundred centimetres of snow fell and our house was completely buried. I lived in a cold and winding house in downtown St John's with three other girls. Grace was on vacation with her family in Thailand and kept sending us videos of her on the beach sipping drinks with umbrellas in them. We told her to stop but she insisted.

The first day wasn't so bad—Franny got really high off a preroll she'd bought from the Tweed store on Water Street and kept reminding us how smart she was for getting weed before the storm. She convinced Lily to share a preroll and Lily started hyperventilating while we watched *Drag Race*. She was losing her mind thinking about how we had no way out and kept telling me that if it came down to it—because my room was only a couple feet from the top of the snowbank—that I would have to jump out the window and start digging. I told her I would, but that didn't regulate her breathing.

I worked at a restaurant downtown and was sleeping on and off with my boss, Rick, who had been my best friend for years. He messaged me first thing after the snowfall saying he slipped a disc shovelling and understood why we were anxious because he would have to spend the next week horizontal. I told him it wasn't exactly the same but he said it was close. His girlfriend, Courtney, was at her parents' house helping them shovel out and Rick was concerned about how he would fill up his Nalgene.

Any time something didn't work out with someone he was dating, Rick would come back to me. He understood that I loved him and wanted to be together but would remind me every time that the stakes were too high—I was too important for him to lose. His dishonesty and flimsiness of character were traits I saw regularly but ignored. It was like I was ski racing and I was getting hit in the face by the red flags over and over again but I just kept going. The girls in the house were unanimous in thinking that Rick had been treating me like shit for years. I'd had frank conversations with them about it before and I would listen to their advice and then would completely exhaust them by ignoring the advice they gave. I could feel myself doing this and it made me feel embarrassed, but that didn't make me stop.

Franny started making cookies and tidying up the living room. Then she rolled out a pie dough while the oven was preheating and I could tell that she was high as a kite. Franny was probably the most anxious one of all of us, but she could hide it when she wanted to.

"I think we should watch all the UK *Love Island* starting at Season One," Franny yelled from the kitchen.

"We've already seen them all," Lily replied. "But the first two are actually so great 'cause they're more real—it's before they started censoring all their behaviour."

"I'm down," I said. "I think it's going to be at least until tomorrow before someone can dig us out."

Lily's phone rang and it was Grace FaceTiming us from Thailand. Grace's sisters were in the background and they were all fighting. Grace was clearly drunk because her eyes were glassy and her cheeks were red. I thought she looked pretty.

"I wish I was there with you guys!" she said. "This is so shit— nothing interesting ever happens in town and I leave and you guys get three days off work trapped in the house."

"We're starting *Love Island* from Season One!" Franny yelled from the kitchen as her timer went off.

"Oh my God, you guys—those are my favourite seasons!"

When we hung up Lily said she wished Grace was there and that something didn't feel right without her. We started watching *Love Island* until it got dark out and I felt slightly panicked that I couldn't leave the situation even if I wanted to. We had finished Franny's cookies and I was desperate for a walk. Rick was messaging me about how he was having a Cronenberg marathon with Courtney and I swear I could have barfed right there and then.

"I don't know, we don't even really talk anymore," Rick texted about Courtney. "It's like we're existing on different planets or something."

I didn't respond but he could see that I'd read the message.

"I don't know, she really wants kids. And I told her I could never do that."

I told Lily and Franny that I was going to the bathroom and I went upstairs and sobbed into my pillow until I heard the *Love Island* theme song downstairs signalling the beginning of a new episode. I grabbed my phone from where I'd left it on my desk and I had eleven missed messages from Rick all saying I'm sorry and asking if that was too much information and how sometimes he didn't know how to navigate our relationship.

"Sorry I don't want you to feel like I'm a shitty guy ... you're so important to me. Really I don't know what I would do without you."

I messaged him back and told him it was fine. "Sorry we're watching *Love Island* and it's seriously insane. I feel like my brain is getting mushy lol."

When I came downstairs my face was red and Franny looked at me and knew I was upset but didn't ask. My relationship with Rick had been hardest on Franny. She'd been there since the start and she understood every contour of it. Franny was the type of person who believed that when she gave advice, people were going to take it. And each time I ignored her and put myself in a position to get hurt, Franny moved slightly further away from me. I could feel it. Each time, I tried to explain by telling her I was a control freak and these things weren't as easy for me as they were for her. I told her she was freer than I was. This time she didn't ask, though.

I had weird dreams all night that I couldn't remember in the morning and I blamed *Love Island*. When I came down the stairs the next morning, Franny was watching *Videodrome* on the TV in the living room and had hung up the wool blankets I had collected since childhood on the large windows so as not to let the light in.

"Rick told me he was watching this last night. He's having a Cronenberg marathon," I said as I sat down on the couch she wasn't using.

"That's cool."

"I was having these weird dreams all night. I think the contrast between like *Love Island* and Snowmageddon has my brain all twisted," I said, biting my thumbnail so short it was painful.

"Did you know all these *Love Island* contestants keep killing themselves? It's all so eerie."

"Dude, can you just let me watch this? It's almost done."

"All right, fine," I said.

I went upstairs and called my mom and told her Franny had pinned my nice blankets to the wall and it made me upset. My mom told me she was worried and detailed some of the crazy storms she'd lived through growing up in Newfoundland.

"Remember what happened to your cousin in Grand Falls? He was out playing in the snow when he was four years old and a snowplow buried him. He was under there for over an hour. And he was fine—I guess he had a little air pocket or something he was breathing through."

"Jesus," I said, even though I knew my mom didn't like it when I used that language.

"This is why I get scared, sweets. You guys have to be careful getting out of your house. Your father and I were watching *Here & Now* and they called in the army to plow the highways, baby."

I promised her we would be careful and that we were fine. I went back downstairs and Franny was at the part of the movie where the videotape is coming out of James Woods's abdomen. The whole thing made me feel hungry.

When Lily came downstairs it was almost noon and she told us that she'd been in her room watching anime and drawing. "I googled *snowmageddon* and it said that *snowpocalypse* and *snowzilla* are also words the press uses to describe storms of massive proportions," she said. "Isn't that funny?"

That's when Franny complained she was running low on weed because she'd smoked so much yesterday and she'd binge-eaten too many cookies and was feeling unbelievably bloated.

She said she missed her boyfriend Ross, who was doing a PhD in Toronto, and she felt alone and scared and trapped. She said she couldn't hear me talk about Rick anymore without losing her mind and that *Love Island* and *Videodrome* and the steady stream of Snowmageddon photos on Instagram had made her brain feel fucked. She said she wanted to do something productive because it was the first time she'd had a few days off work but she couldn't concentrate on anything so she'd bought a small top with strings you wrap around the back from Aritzia for 120 dollars.

I reminded her she would never wear a top like that in town and she started crying and said, "I know okay," so loudly it almost bounced off the walls.

"I need to get out of here," she said between laboured breaths. "Someone needs to get us out of here." I knew she meant the house but I thought something bigger was going on. I wanted to be a better friend to her but I was barely hanging on myself. I wanted to tell her about my cousin surviving in the air pocket after getting buried with snow but I didn't think it would help.

Lily's boyfriend Jonathan came to dig us out that afternoon and three other neighbours pitched in to help. I watched them from my bedroom window and was happy I hadn't tried to jump. Jonathan created a tunnel to the road and we kept it that way for a week because it was funny.

*

The day after we were freed, Rick asked me if I wanted to go to the Golden Phoenix on Kenmount for all-you-can-eat buffet. At this point we had talked so much since the comment about him and Courtney having kids that I'd convinced him—and maybe myself—that it was all okay. The drive to Golden Phoenix in Rick's Corolla was dicey at best and we slid for half a block coming down Freshwater. When we got there I had more food than I'd had in ages and chalked it up to a scarcity mindset given rationing while the city was shut down.

"I think Franny's mad at me," I told Rick as I shoved a chicken ball in my mouth in one bite.

"Franny's a bit temperamental. She'll be okay," Rick said.

I thought it was rich that he would be calling anyone else temperamental but I didn't say anything. I just made an mmm sound like I agreed with him. "How was the Cronenberg marathon after?"

"It was all right. Courtney got grossed out when the guy's head explodes in *Scanners* so she made me turn on something else."

I laughed and secretly wished he would stop talking to me about Courtney.

"I don't know, she just doesn't really understand or appreciate body horror," Rick said. He had some red sauce by his mouth and it looked like blood almost. "Did you ever notice if you look up the ceiling here it's painted like the sky?"

I looked up and appreciated it for what felt like minutes. The gold light fixtures hung down in the middle of the sky.

"I think it's kind of beautiful," Rick said.

"Really?" I lowered my head and looked at him. "It makes me feel trapped."

Joel Thomas Hynes

NOTHING BUT A LEGACY

Full dark out now. It's been warm and there's still a few flies, but Dad says how he can smell winter in the air. Like as if winter had some sort of smell to itself that showed up before the other stuff—the cold and the slush and the snow and ice.

That's it now, he goes, you can smell it.

Mom is gone down the harbour for the bingo games. I wanted to go with her, but I wasn't allowed. Dad is here at the table with me. We're playing eights. He could have laid that queen two turns ago. I don't mind. He's drinking his Black Horse. On his fifth bottle. I've been counting. This one is almost gone and when he takes his last sip, before the bottle touches back down on the table, I'll be already to the fridge and back again with number six. That's how fast I am. But then that's it for our game, once the beer is all gone.

Dad glances at the clock again. Lukey was supposed to be back almost an hour ago. He got his driver's test tomorrow, Lukey. So he's supposed to be home and not out sniffin around. That's what Dad says he's at, sniffin around, making trouble.

Mark is in the backroom watching the Jays game with Marissa. Every time there's the roar from the announcer, Dad shouts in to ask what happened, who caught that one, who hit that one, who came in. Mark or Marissa don't ever answer. I don't think they're paying much attention to the game. I think they're sucking face, or worse. Don't think I don't know what worse is neither. Worse is what I saw when I ran into Mark's room last week. I saw Marissa's boob out of her shirt. Mark was lying on the bed and she was sitting on top of him. They were sucking face and when I ran into the room Marissa squealed and jumped back and I saw her boob. I saw the nipple on the end. I did, I saw it. Brian out the road says you can see every inch of flesh on a girl's chest, but if you don't see the nipple then it don't count. The nipple makes the boob. Mark threw a green lighter at me and just missed my head but I didn't leave the room. He shouted:

Get out ya little perv!

But I still couldn't move.

Marissa covered herself up but I could still see her boob in my mind. The picture burned into my head, like when you looks at a light bulb and then tries to look at something else. When she smiled and said:

Okay John-John, you move along now.

That's when I left. Her voice is nice and soft.

*

Dad glares at the clock, gets up and parts the curtains above the sink, cups his hands around his face and presses his nose to the glass. He stands there like that, looking out across the track in the direction Lukey made off earlier this evening.

Fuckin legacy. Nothing but a fuckin legacy.

That's what Dad calls Lukey and Mark when they're not doing what they should be doing—a legacy. He's never said I was one, but sometimes Mark does. I keep meaning to look it up because I'm pretty sure I'm not one.

Yesterday Lukey taught me how to trap a tomcat. One medium-sized cardboard box, one paint stick, a long piece of string, and a plate of tinned ham. He made me swear not to tell we took the ham from the house. The box is set upside down and propped up at one end with the paint stick. Lukey tied the string to the bottom end of the stick and set the plate of ham on the ground under the box. Then we sat on the step and waited for a cat. Lukey sent me in to get a cigarette from Mom's package on the table. Then he let me hold the string attached to the stick. We sat and waited. I didn't know what was going to happen. Then came the Ryans' ragged orange tomcat and got a whiff of what was on the plate. He went in the box and sat in front of the plate and growled and ate. We watched him for a while, waited and watched. Finally Luke told me to pull the string and I did and the box fell on the cat, only not completely over him. It landed on his bum and tail and the cat went berserk, howling and scratching and tryna get away, but he only managed to trap himself underneath the box altogether. Then he howled really loud from inside the box. It was a sad and spooky sound. Luke threw a rock and hit the box and tipped it so the cat took off. Half the ham was gone. We set the box up again and went back to the step and waited, but no more cats came.

Lukey says in the fall, when the frost comes, if he's still here, he'll show me how to snare a rabbit. He says we'll keep the rabbits and eat them. I don't know. I tell Lukey how I don't much care for eating a dead rabbit. He laughs and says:

Would you rather eat a live one?

I hope Lukey's still here when the frost comes. Mark is moving out to Kilbride to go fixing cars with Uncle Charlie. If Lukey goes off too, that'll mean just me and Dad and Mom. Mom don't talk much. I ask Lukey if I can eat a rabbit with ketchup and he says yes, so I says well I'll *try* one. That means he'll have to be around to catch one for me.

*

Dad tosses his hand into the pile in the middle of the table and belches. He's finished with the cards now. He stands and upends the rest of his Black Horse and walks across the kitchen to fetch the last one out of the fridge himself. He's gone sour now. He tromps out to the back porch, opens the door, and stands there staring out the track, chugging his beer. It's pitch-black and the wind is up. We are the last house right out at the end of the track. There's nothing out here except hills and woods and rocks. Dad stands in the doorway, mumbling under his breath. Lukey done something bad last week and the police brought him home. He was not too steady on his legs. When the cop left, Dad told me to get upstairs and I did and listened from the top of the stairs at them shouting and swearing for a long time. Dad can get pretty loud. Then there was a big bang and something smashed and Mom started crying and I ran into my room when I heard Lukey coming up the stairs. Lukey and me are in the same room and Mark has his own room. Lukey's lip was bleeding and he pressed a sock to it. He didn't answer when I asked him how he cut his lip. He stank like beer. He told me the police think he went to school when he wasn't supposed to be there. He said they think he went there in the nighttime with some friends, when school was closed. The police took his boots from the porch. Lukey says they're gonna try and make a plaster of the bottoms of his shoes, and then try to match the pattern with footprints they found in the school. He says it'll never work though. I asks why not. He reaches under the bed and pulls out his ratty old sneakers:

'Cause I was wearing these ones.

He laughs and hands me his cigarette to hold while he takes his sweater off. I watches the blue-grey smoke curl up around my elbow. Lukey sees me watching the cigarette.

Go ahead, he says, take a little draw…

Elise Levine

///////////

COOLER

I interview Friday afternoon, Saturday morning buy the pants—the pleats, that crease. The wedge shoes with arch support, and a good thing too. That night I clock miles over the blue-and-gold carpet, resting the dogs only in the marble-clad stalls of the ladies' restrooms where I briefly lose the clanging slots, the high rollers' yips and groans—one of my new job's perks is that I never have to steal away to the basement and bless the employee can.

I learn fast: no strolling or loitering when a player runs serious hot. Dan or Gustavo or Cynthia tips forefinger to brow and I amble over to the big table and ask in. Don't let on that my chips belong to the house. Strike up an unassuming convo with the rocketeer and dampen the sparks. Not that I'm cheating or distracting—my mere presence does the trick.

Nothing crackles from me. My luck? Failure to win. Killjoy, my parents taunted whenever the fam played crazy eights and I cried over my starter kitty of ten pennies going and gone. Sad Sack Samantha, Mom and Dad would jeer. World's sorest loser! By age ten I knew that stoic resignation was my best if not my only bet.

Until I met Deb and levelled up. Got my awareness raised.

My one and only old flame. She who trafficked in multi-dimensional high-frequency attunements and how they flow. Or don't, in my case.

I miss her. She failed to tear my heart out, but it was complicated nonetheless.

We met cute one rainy afternoon two weeks ago. I, Assistant Stockist at Shop Smart, twenty-four years of age and newly barely degreed in Business Comm with a Marketing concentration, and so with little hope hoping to move the dial on my fortune in the world, uncharacteristically threw caution to the wind and abandoned my post stacking gum and candy bars to help scan her Tofutti—a product new to me and the store—at the self-checkout. She was something, in her purple tee-dress and yellow flip-flops and crystal pendant necklace, and I don't know what came over me, some sudden notion I had to for once seize the day—*carpe diem* ironically coming easily to mind, being my former high school's motto, which pretty much had never pertained to me—when out of nowhere she pulled an eerie pre-empt by asking me out for matcha when my shift ended. Me, matcha! In no time we were at the café next door in the strip mall, a place I'd previously eyed but frankly been too intimidated to try. She reached across the wobbly café table to straighten my twisted polo collar, leaned close, and swore she could see my muddy aura spike pastel peach. A smidge, she said, nothing razzle-dazzle—she liked to keep things real.

That very evening we spooned on her couch—spooned!—and straight away it was all hard on me, not what I was used to. Winning for a change. It made my jaw ache, my feet itch.

What's up? she asked when I crawled onto her carpet and curled on my side.

I spilled the uncool beans. She sat up straight with her arms folded and a frown on her face.

Maybe slip into something more comfortable?

With some coaxing I shrugged off my shirt and she disappeared into her bedroom and returned bearing a satiny bathrobe, freshly laundered, as she explained.

I donned the garment. But I who found it taxing to make it to my neighbourhood Soap Opera Quick Wash once a week immediately succumbed to the worst rash.

A soothing shower?

At her urging—try a new look for the new you!—I ran her blow-dryer to straighten my habitually tangled curls. Clumps dropped to the floor.

Forget stoic. I moped. I cried. I lost sleep that night and the next—downgraded to a miserly seven hours a night. I grumbled about my fatigue like an old coot.

So much for new, I believe I moaned.

And so, three days into the cuddle-doves, she announced her imminent departure on a major as in never-coming-back-from trip. Which she kindly claimed she'd been planning to do for a while. Something about needing desert and red rock and starseeds and the alchemy of ascension to salve the damages a lifetime of betrayals and poor-sport-ness had done her—the latter an attitude I apparently owned. Wounds I'd at the very least neglected to fix.

She told me this huddled over kombucha shots at the café I now—on this my second visit, pre- my next shift at the store—considered our place while I studied the green gunk on the inside of my glass.

Go ahead, she urged me in a tone so sweet my teeth hurt. Get your grump back on, she understood, no way would she take it personally. And did I know the local casino could use help like mine? Which, alas, she could not.

Customers came and went, placing orders at the counter, hefting hips onto stools by the window which looked out onto our mini-mall's parking lot, people parking, departing. All was motion, change. Except I couldn't move. Could. Not. She took my hand, which felt like someone else's. On second thought, it felt like just mine. Like how mine always felt—like it was embarrassed to belong to luckless me.

She flashed a smile big on the gums and I revived enough to tell her no worries, it was okay, I got it.

Her smile sagged and she sighed and said the rest would be her one-way to Phoenix.

Whereas you—and here her voice took on this whispery, seer-like tone that quivered the hair on my arms—you, Sad Sack Samantha, Wilmington born and bred, will forever stay.

And so it was revealed: I at least had a gift I could cash in.

Which led this bored Shop Smarter to get their rear in gear and land this better-paying, way more interesting gig.

*

With my third paycheque I bankroll more perma-press. The months pile on and the sensible shoes wear out, but I never mess with the style. What works works. A year clicks over and, still thinking of Deb—the hippie drama with which she dressed, her free-spiritedness—I brave a splash-out. The blouses upgrade from cotton-poly to lyocell, beige to pale pink and royal blue. Everything no-iron, but no prints, no way. I hold my breath—and keep my job. Further emboldened, I add in the aspirational knock-off purse. Spring for clear polish on the nails. Hair done a medium wavy bob that covers the bald patches from my unfortunate episode with Deb's dryer, then every six weeks a lob back to bob, and so forth, with humble highlights kicked in.

Not that anyone will notice. Which is the point: that I fly under the cosmic-vibe radar. Which is tough. Herein lies my dilemma: it sucks that my job suits me like silk. That my modest good luck, being my kind of luck, might scram.

*

Minutes to midnight on a royal-blue Tuesday, I've just returned from bathroom break and there at the blackjack is something so far-out else I wonder if even Deb could have foreseen it.

The auburn hair in a loose updo. Fat onyx studs agleam in seashell ears. A gauzy red capelet floating about the shoulders of a black sheath. The silvery laugh at each blown hand and shivery hiccups upon tossing back each comped drink. At each fold the clapping like a kid giddy on Kool-Aid, the bracelets circling her wrists offering a festive tambourine shake.

She's down three grand. Five, seven. She's grand. Even Gustavo smiles.

As per my job at the casino, I keep it cool. A crowd has gathered, but what's the deal? She's just another loser, just like me. Maybe on a more exalted, next-level scale—a whale of a loser—but so?

I keep it sour. How come she gets to live so large? When here I am, months into antacids for dinner at my growing fear that each treasured work night might be my last—odds are things will go south, I can practically count on it. Worse—something to do with the whale, I think, near-hypnotized by a certain pull on me, this tightening, lengthening, this perking in parts including but not limited to my heart and which I try my best to ignore, woefully aware of the little that's ever come of the experience—I find myself momentarily helpless to recount a representative sample of my lifelong chill-pills.

Deb's piled-on pity at Karma Kombucha, for one. For two: Franny Taggert's snort when, at age twelve, trying to impress her, I split my lip from a botched twirl at the skating rink. For three: why not Danny Rogelman's *fat chance* piped at me in front of our tittering grade nine French class after I slipped the note asking him to prom. Four: in college, Maya Chu's toothpaste-y *what the?* when I nuzzled her ear at student union movie night—Bergman's *Persona* ever since reminding me of a two-mile solo return walk through freezing sleet to our cinder-block dorm.

Do I know cold. And while I break my heart again for each old time's sake, the whale burns wads with such joy a damp fire swamps my bones.

At five in the morning she finally packs it in. And, just as I'd bet she would, lays upon the dealer one lit tip.

*

For days I hardly sleep and nights she's a no-show until Tuesday rolls around again and, blessedly still on the job, I'm witness to another whale of a show and the crowd she draws.

I survey her table from afar until I can't take it any longer— her air of victory at each triumphant loss, the brutal thrill that now streaks through me—and go warm a seat in one of the fancy bathrooms, checking off-brand sales on my phone while randos shuffle in and out of the surrounding stalls. Which kills me, I have all the feels and all the questions—but such is life when the whys and hows are not for pity-parties like me.

The end of my shift finally draws nigh. Figuring the coast might be clear on the floor, the crowds hushed back to their homes, I flush and open.

There she is, exiting the stall next door.

We stop short and stare. Is she tall. Gangly arms and legs poke out of a swingy, swirly colour number. Pretty sure I'm now gawking, from this close up I realize she's too damned thin. As if, despite her élan, her writ-largeness with the big flop—because of it? the cost such brio exacts?—something's super wrong.

I think: warm plates of box mac 'n' cheese, steaming bowls of instant ramen. Dishes I can actually sort of cook.

I think of Deb, offering a split-second prayer of gratitude for her role in leading me to this moment—an instant in which I'm also aware I might never think of Deb again.

As if the whale can read my thoughts, she flirt-tilts her chin.

Heat rises in my throat and face, not entirely pleasant. Okay, somewhat pleasant. Very confusing. Me, blush?

She raises a bony finger to her lips.

Between us, she says.

*

I clock out at seven in the morning and by seven thirty we're holding hands in the front seat of her Fit. Having made out, sort of, given the size of her car. Something unfamiliar bubbles in my gut. I'm— What am I? What is she? We? Happy as—

Candy? she says, withdrawing her hand to offer a breath mint.

We chew and suck in silence then she starts the car and pilots us out of the underground lot. Leaving my ancient Sentra's fate to the mercy of the towing gods, who usually can't resist harshing those of my ilk—but I'm all, What? Me worry now?

Twenty minutes later, she pulls over in front of my apartment building and I ask her in. She leans over and kisses me once more. My chest thrums, my head, between my legs. She is a mystery at heart and so am I. And it's cool. And maybe I'm cool, first time for everything—until a freak niggle hooks me, a tiny insistent worm, and, dumdum that I am, I bite.

Where's it all coming from? I ask.

The money, is what I'm thinking—blundering past my churning thoughts of sex, power, powerful sex, me and her forever. Blindly thinking more, in this moment—in accordance with the tedious precepts of my schooling—of how to make the stone-coldest buy-in of my life.

She withdraws into her seat and forward-faces.

Um, yeah, she says. Just some clients.

I should have known: as if I could press my luck as if I had her buckets to spend. Now I can count on the big N.O. to my as yet unasked question, the one about coming inside—never mind my studio sublet's a haz-mat zone. The big ask with the oversize sub-text: *Care to join me in fanning what might-could turn into an eternal flame?*

And yet my yearning soul remains split.

Clients. The word orbits my brain.

How do you find these dopes? I blurt, figuring I've blown it with her anyway and now have nothing left to lose.

She peruses me a long moment. A wavelet of excitement laps my throat. I gulp it in and, greedy for more, hold her gaze.

Oh ho, she says evenly. Easy, tiger. Not so fast.

I do it anyway—desperate now, in full recognition of my initial breach, I rewind, I show her fast. I'm sorry, my mistake, I get it—and when can I see her again? Movie date. Bistro dinner. Sunset stroll along the pinkening beach. Shelter for two under a single blanket while the horseshoe crabs mate under the full moon. No? No? Shared snoot of gin from a flask during my break next Tuesday at the casino. Side-by-side swings on the swings in a park in her neighbourhood—where did she say she lived?

She hisses a cold breath. Reaches across to open my door, arm grazing my breasts. I gasp, arch my back—okay, yes! I could go again, why not? But she withdraws her arm and nudges my shoulder, hard, with hers.

I shrink in my seat. Okay, I get it, really I do!

Though I don't, not any of it. Not me and her. Not the apparent business she's apparently in. But okay, okay. Okay! No argument from me.

She tootles off. I stand as if glued to the sidewalk. And then, within half a block, she hits the brakes and reverses with a squeal. Behind me a car horn honks, someone heading the right way along the one way. The driver shakes their fist. The whale— my first, my only whale!—swerves even with me and buzzes down the window on my side while the car behind us wails.

I lean in. Grey eyes, somehow-elegant pimple to the left of her off-centre, regal nose. I wonder when she'd found time to reapply her red lipstick, the exact shade, I notice now, of her cape. Her lips part once more, and my breath catches like some creature— some hitherto hidden something, a thing I can't possibly know what—shocked to suddenly surface mid-air.

We're something, she says, as if she's sort-of, kind-of read my mind. Really something.

*

I snap the blackout curtains shut. Take off my pants and shoes and blouse. Unusual for me, I hang what needs hanging and line up what needs aligning. And then pace in circles, a strange fizz in my fingertips, my knees. My tongue where it fished hers. Clients. Something. My brain burns. Between you and me. Like we share a secret or we're the secret. And who would I tell—tell what? I lie on the bed. It spins or I do. Like a roulette wheel—I can't help the cringe-y thought—twirling for all the little I'm worth as her red cape flutters in my dazed head. I press my own finger to my own lips. Somehow they're spinning too. For all the little I'm worth—or is it, might it be, the more?

*

Two weeks drudge by, no whale. Such is my life and such will it ever be: my upsides my downsides.

Still, I order a half-dozen shrink-wrapped twenty-packs of breath mints online, next-day delivery, and chew and suck as if they might return her. Two more weeks pass then two more. And then two by two they come, until a year and then another sails past. I buy more same-old pants and blouses and shoes. But, and: I make a habit of hanging my things in the closet and aligning the condiment bottles on the fridge shelves. And it all looks pretty good, everything in its place. That third winter my hair grows out enough to entirely cover my bald patches, the ones from when I tried the blow-dryer in so-and-so's bathroom—I realize this sounds cruel, but who even was that anyway? And though once again I go about my days and nights slow and steady like I'm walking on eggshells, now it all feels like something, an accumulation of somethings that together might-could make a larger something, a thing that can't be rushed.

Until spring returns and I say duck it. Purchase a slim-fit shirt with scarlet pinstripes—scarlet!—and hold my breath as spring roars to summer. And, defying fate, live to tell the tale. Tuck a sturdy grin beneath my professional placid mien: accept that a job neatly done is just my style. Work or home, I risk believing I've at last drawn my numbers in the lottery of longings.

Another new year begins.

At the casino the flyers continue to up, up, and away on successive hands, the air thinning until they're north of nowhere anyone should ever be—in grave danger, I've come to believe, of losing themselves in the quivering frequencies of pure light.

And it's okay, I've got them. I, their minty-breathed friend in time of need, lift too, swanning through the graces of my lucklessness by virtue of my mere proximity at the gaming tables—my low-fi vibe enough to fish them back to a place not too hot, not too cold. Like me: just right.

Things look up in other ways too.

Don't ask me how—I'm a newcomer to this special game, but my best bet is word of mouth, insider knowledge passed along— and also don't inquire about the long-term cost-benefit, keeping in mind the possible personal price my now lost-to-me whale paid, and for sure don't wonder aloud where the blazes she went to in the end, if it was a case of she got out of the racket altogether or found fairer seas elsewhere, but anyway: whatever the reasons and whatever the qualms, what's not to be beat is, I'm needed and appreciated more than ever here.

Last night alone, on three separate occasions, players slipped me their business cards. Handwritten on their backs in tiny lettering, a certain now-trending plea.

Call, the clients-in-waiting implore. Name your price. Save us, please.

Sourayan Mookerjea

LONG HAUL

Jeff snarled as he swung his bull-headed axe through the door. The blow pulled apart the hinges like broken fingers hanging on to the frame. He kicked the door over with his ash-covered, stubby steel-toed boots and leaned in. He waved over his shoulder to his partner Kim to follow and swivelled their searchlight into the gloom. Thick, dark smoke hung and swayed in folds and curtains down the hallway and the light beam sparked swarming fireflies as they stepped out of the raging blizzard of ash outside into the quiet dark. The fire had ripped through the new subdivision with the sudden ferocity of a drone strike out of the dead of night. Jeff and Kim were with the first crew to arrive at the installation by helicopters scrambled from the airport at Fort McMurray after the explosions. The two firefighters waded cautiously down the hallway. Jeff held his axe out in front of him and Kim followed a step behind until Jeff tripped on something and Kim slammed into his oxygen tanks, knocking him forward. The slashing beam of light revealed a big padded boot and a pile of children's snowsuits and more winter footgear scattered down the hall. Kim pulled him up by the arms and they set forward again until a skateboard arced up out of a stream of smoke and bit Jeff on the kneecap and clattered loudly back into the fuming depths. He swore, grabbed his knee, and pulled Kim in front of him and gave her a push to make her lead the way. She looked over her shoulder and saw sullen anger, so she stepped forward, with deliberation, raising her arms in front of her as if they were moving through a tai chi set in the soot-billowed tranquility of the hallway. Fifteen, maybe twenty, slow, unfurling steps later their searchlight caught the edge of a flat screen twisted off its arm bent over in prayer. Jeff turned the light upward and around. They now seemed to be in a large room. The clotted smoke was thicker here. A wall blistered upward with streaking fangs of soot without reaching a ceiling, but on the way their passing light uncloaked a human figure suspended from the wall. A helmet and visor, some kind of full-body armour, both alien and medieval, with plumage and chain mail, then it was gone. The zigzags of light couldn't find it again. Instead, floating in a void, the spider legs and torso of a chandelier bejewelled with sparkling teeth and flashbulb eyes burst into fireworks and swayed gently, though they felt no trace of a breeze in the glacial smoke. Turning around, the moonbeam of light now climbed over the stainless steel rib cages of a modular sofa set, along the blackened dials and levers and pumps and steam engines of an espresso bar fronting a marbled kitchenette, past the charcoal corpse of a grand piano and a tiger-striped model heavy-hauler dispensing oxygen shots and vitamin water, to the magnificent head of an elk mounted over the granite fireplace, its antlers growing like an arbutus into the dark clouds. They shuffled their way through this playground snowed with ash, cautiously feeling their way

to the first room off the second hallway. Kim pushed the door open with her toe. Was it a child's bedroom? Clothes and toys were strewn everywhere in molten, charred disorder, drawers and closets tipped and gutted and whirled in a tornado. The long, toothy grin of a dog's charcoal skull greeted her from under the smouldering bed, tail wagging, until the spinning room dissolved into powder and she heard a loud bang through the fist of dust before she leaped into utter darkness and felt a freight train run over her forever. When the silence returned, as abruptly, time kept passing, Kim felt, through the darkness on the other side of her visor while her beating heart drummed inside her helmet like a jackhammer.

This is good, she heard herself say, feeling very thirsty.

As the whirling dust storm began to thin, she could see a small, bobbing disc of light in the distance, even with her eyes closed, it seemed. She felt a gurgling cough and realized that Jeff was behind her, leaning against her back. They were both seated, their knees up against their chests, too tightly, it felt. Jeff fumbled for the searchlight, found it, and tried the switch. Somehow it worked. They were caught in a small, miraculous space where two bedroom walls had caved into each other, they figured, protecting them from the beam or floor or whatever it was that had given way and fallen around them. She felt the pull of the halo of light strongly as if it was coiling around her.

We have to get out, she said.

That's an idea.

No, I mean we *have* to get out.

Can you even move?

She hurt everywhere, but she could move, she thought.

Maybe if we can get through the drywall, Jeff asked.

Let's go.

Leaning back against Jeff, using him as a springboard, she jumped forward at the wall and, after the third kick, got into a rhythm, praying that nothing else would fall, until her boots broke through and she was out to her hips. She wriggled out, turned over, and reached back to pull Jeff through. Half the building had collapsed, it looked like, but the tennis ball of light bounced down the first hallway they took coming in. They scrambled as quickly as they could on hands and knees, past the fireplace, past the elk's head glaring at them from a pile of rubble, down the hall, following the ball of light, out to the door flashing yellow from the emergency lights on their truck outside.

The storm of ash was still blowing strong, and beyond the chimneys and beams of the mansions and estates in the torched subdivision, the horizon to the west glowed orange. At the truck, they turned the headlights on, strode into its flood, and looked at each other carefully. Jeff was grinning and pitched his glove, fastball, at Kim's head. She dodged, caught it over her shoulder, and was about to toss it into the cab when their radios buzzed again. The control room wanted everyone at the reactors on the far edge of town. Kim threw the gauntlet in Jeff's lap and took the wheel. They wound their way out of the subdivision along empty roads, occasionally passing abandoned pickup trucks and delivery vans, and turned onto the highway into town. The falling ash was so thick now that Kim had to kill the headlights to be able to see the road. The running lights and flashers turned the ash into beating wings of gold soaring over the drifting pavement. Inside the cab, they had taken their helmets off. Jeff studied Kim's dark, tired, and worried face. They had first crossed paths more than fifteen years ago during tumultuous times. The never-ending pandemic had unleashed another variant of concern, leaving the suite of vaccines useless and striking with merciless virulence those without hideouts. This time, strikes and demonstrations reached a fever pitch of anger. He had met her for the first time at the union hall. The meetings were tense and she spoke with purpose and force. He ran into her again at a training session, glistening with honey, on the cables at the climbing wall. They had spent the summer and fall on the picket lines and in the committees together, and he had wanted her like a cigarette. Then in the winter things got complicated. Deals were done and, in the end, the local closed its doors. Kim's whole crew got flexed. He remembered her eyes sparking clarity, her voice sharp as the blade of his axe at the meeting where all the non-white workers walked out in protest. Jeff was among the lucky few, grandfathered and specialized to protect critical infrastructure against land defender activity in the boonies. They had only been on a few sites together in all those years of unceasing orange alerts and yeah, things were kind of awkward for everyone ever since, so nobody let it get in the way of the job, and it was safer that way anyways. He knew she had a lot of people depending on her and so did he, so he wasn't going to bring up the past. And without the local, everything had changed in the meantime. The work, the crews, the command, the structure. But *this* was something else, totally. They had never seen anything like this, ever.

They were nearing the edge of town. Above the treeline on the hills they could make out great vortices of ash where the angelic swords of the windmills were still turning in the fallout, lighting themselves up like gaseous spiral galaxies. Kim found the turnoff by the big-box outlets and took the parkway that linked the sprawling e-waste shipping depot to the village centre. They now had to navigate around clusters of abandoned robots on the road, frozen in mid-manoeuvre, lifting, turning, drilling as if they had escaped from their sheds and had been left out for the night like the cranes and excavators in their pens along the side of the road. Their radios sputtered out of the void once more. They were to go to Gate D. Kim looked at Jeff.

D or B? Last time they said B.

Yeah, pretty sure they did.

Jeff pressed the call button. Nothing. He held it pressed while Kim pulled into the townsite. Fort Jasper. Where Las Vegas married into Los Angeles to upmarket the Canadian Crown Jewels, "the frontier of the new economy" the tag line went. They had logged an excuse to avoid the perimeter highway just to see it. The great lunar pox scars of the tar sands and their vast reservoirs and flood plains of toxic tailing slurry had been finally scabbed over and buried by the very funerary medicine that had long been clawed out and stripped from the living forest soil. One hundred and forty-two thousand square kilometres of algorithmically fertile national park–themed wilderness in proprietary extruded metamorphic bitumen from the bear shit to glaciers and the carbon credit boreal forest that nested the eco-village of condos, casinos, and tech campuses, while the mines had fled deeper into the subterranean folds of the earth's ancient crust. The main street of this supersized, public-private, stolen candy-land was dark and quiet. Living walls cloaked the hotels right up to their rooftop gardens, where owls hooted at the bestiary of exotic logos prowling the streets below them for their next meal. Beyond them, the turrets of earth-ships slunk through the Astroturf and the gingerbread croft houses on the golf courses foraged in the shadows. The glistening bitumen-sheathed palisade of the Canadian Tire Spirit Lodge visitor centre towered above them all. Ever since they had left the helicopters at the muster station—Kim hit the brakes hard, then ran the red light— they had not come across a single soul anywhere.

Where did they all go?

There must be shelters, they're playing it safe, must be.

Or taken out by the Warrior Underground already...

The radio buzzed back D. Last time they definitely said B. Boston. Barracuda. But this was the control room in the centre block. Jeff was scratching his head. Kim drummed the steering wheel. They didn't need the politics. Centre block, they figured, probably outranked the dispatch station, or maybe it was an algorithm thing. They would decide when they got there, they agreed. Kim turned left onto another access road back out toward the perimeter leading to the nuclear reactors on the far side of the ridge of berms. The reactors were the anchors that were sunk into rock to hold everything together: the miraculous mix of energy sources that gave the world its unprecedented bituminous plasticity, as though decay had been conquered and mummified into a new infinity by its coagulated fetal blood. Fort Jasper was the undisputed capital of this dawning empire, more famous than the old Fort, now by far the cheaper option an hour down the highway, had ever been. But just as notorious. People either hated or loved Fort Jasper. She knew a few people who moved there, all young people in a hurry to go big. Her daughter had for a time dated a green and frantic boy who had worked his way from a golf course to a casino before fading away. Kim was thinking how that had happened to everyone she knew, though. Her people were from all around the relentless turns of the river there, though her parents had moved to Edmonton when they were young, and she had grown up in the city. All those years and those people had moved on, she didn't know where, their muddy tracks in the gravel mined out, their houses bulldozed, their children sent to more flashing, mercurial fates. Kim stepped harder on the gas, climbing the ridge, as a familiar hunger woke in the pit of her stomach and started gnawing at whatever it could remember. Her own children, she thought again, were in exactly the same boat. She worried about her daughter the most, sharp but reckless, but the boys too had no reliable connections for the long haul. They had all done everything right at school and with their sheaves of degrees and certificates they all picked up work when they could, construction, office work, online piecework sorting and matching, or cleaning machines at the hospital, but nothing lasted long, so they all ended up back with her. The people left behind by the dawn of the Age of Aquarius, she said to Jeff, are just the people in the way of the Age of Aquarius. He looked over, startled by the abrupt fortune cookie. The engine was revving violently as they neared the crest of the ridge.

Is that the Slaughter House Pigs? he asked, trying to sound in the know, but slurring his words with too much teeth into some fake accent.

Who?

You know, the Slaughter House Pigs.

She gave him a look and scowled. Going over the top, they fell into what seemed like a blazing autumn birch forest lifted shimmering in a sudden rapture of sunset until the wind scattered the fireball and the fluorescent flares and thunderheads of catastrophe blinked and flashed in the sharp stench of burning plastic and overheated metal. A bright blue-and-white diagram of the complex approached out of the thick ash and pointed toward D, the first turnoff, so they took it and found the gates at the end of a freshly painted road, and then the parking lot, nearly full with trucks, their yellow lights flashing like a field of lighthouses.

"Over here!" Jeff barked. Kim saw the empty spot and pulled in. "We're late!" Jeff barked again, as if their detour through the townsite had been entirely her idea. They strapped on their helmets, hoisted their packs on, and ran to the first blue door in the steel shed protruding into the parking lot, went in, and joined the line at the very back.

The large shed felt close and hot as the line snaked around and up four ramps on either side of a stage with large riveted steel jaws clenched against the inferno beyond them. The briefing had already started and was hard to make out through the microphone static, but they knew the basics from the airlift. One of the reactors had lost power—did they say now, unit three?—overheated, and the explosions started the fires. Their job was to put them out and restart the pumps to cool the rods to keep the rest of the complex from going into runaway meltdown. The man with the tidy grey haircut and wax face, wearing gold spectacles in full uniform at the podium, then turned to explain the catch, pointing with his laser at a map of the installation on a large monitor at the far end of the shed. The only water available to them anywhere was from the reactor cooling system since the carbon capture and sequestration plant and the mines the generator powered had drained all the lakes and aquifers years ago. They could live with the fallout from dirty water, mission control had decided, rather than risk more explosions. The red ball of laser light was bouncing from reactor to reactor as the fire chief laid out strategy. There were six reactors in all, each making steam to drive turbines, one powering Fort Jasper, two powering the carbon capture plant, and the rest powering the bitumen mines. One crew would go to pipe water, another to fight the fires, and a third to fix the pumps so water in the coolant baths would circulate and keep the rods from overheating. For this they would need to bootstrap the steam-driven turbines to generate enough electricity to run the pumps. The reactors were still turning water into steam, theoretically, for the turbines, for the mines, and for the sequestration pumps injecting the sludge of captured carbon and nuclear waste into the void of abandoned wells and ancient empty aquifers. But each reactor was designed to compete with each other for the water it turned into steam and for the water it used to cool itself with to optimize the performance of each turbine for its current load. Just the pumps themselves, Jeff had marvelled in the helicopter, were like a fleet of battleships plying the currents of this underground sea, never mind the reactors they were armed with. No one was sure how the whole dragon would react to them pulling on its wires and rerouting its pipes to get its powerful heart to beat again with pacific control. But they had no choice, the Chief exclaimed with tight red circles throbbing on the map, until the ministry worked out the legalities and prices of drawing emergency power downstream from the grid, they were going in to do "the hard and dirty work this great nation was built with."

"Running for office, that one," Kim snickered at the Chief's tacked-on oratory. Jeff tugged at her elbow, wanting to work on the big pumps, but they were at the back of the line and got directed toward the ramp to the reservoirs by brisk supervisors with clipboards and blue overalls already in position to wrangle the operation. Everyone was quiet, shuffling forward in turn, weighted by the enormity of what they were expected to do. Jeff went silent and kept his oxygen pack turned back toward Kim. At their turn at the deployment desk, the foreman, arguing with someone on his phone, didn't see them and walked away and out through a door. There was no gear left for them on the table so they followed the others up the ramp, through a set of double doors, and down a long, zigzagging corridor, with blue-and-red emergency lights unfolding the way. After a while they noticed that the corridor was leading downward, steeper at every turn, and Kim wondered what it was that was turning them this way and that. The air was now hot and thick and they were sweating profusely in their heavy fire suits. They turned again, more sharply, and the floor was now a steel gangway that swayed reverberantly with their millipede stamping footsteps and they could hear rushing water through the walls. A strong, hot wind picked up suddenly and charged at them down the corridor, blowing, Kim thought, red flowers all over them until she turned very cold. The rushing water was getting unbearably loud, banging the walls with thunderous force so that the vibrations made it difficult to see or breathe. The red, fleshy flowers seemed to be growing everywhere, on the walls, on the ramp, on Jeff's back, on the tips of Kim's fingers. How did they end up at the front of the line, Kim thought, feeling sure all the others were now trudging along behind her. She tried to look back, but her goggles were now stained by the red flesh so she couldn't see past Jeff's bobbing helmet either. The smell of burning flesh made her retch and a strong metallic taste furred her tongue. Right away Kim realized that the thunderous clanging was not water but the toxic carboniferous sludge vomiting out of the entrails of the explosions and slithering all around them. She tried to read the them what she had glimpsed through the elevator window, unintelligibly and unbelievably, she couldn't tell if she wasn't able to speak, her mouth moulded into some bit of metal, or whether they couldn't hear her through the clattering din of the falling elevator. They were oblivious, talking excitedly about something she couldn't hear. She looked for Jeff, but now the elevator cab was dark and with their helmets, reflective bands, and heavy suits she could not tell him apart. In this light you would have to get pretty close, too close for these guys, she was thinking, when the elevator jerked and then fell hundreds of feet, she felt, before jerking again, then resuming its calculated descent just as their radios crackled to life. "I want you men to know," a voice seated in a polished oak carriage rolled into the elevator cab, "that this mission you are on is the most important thing you will ever do in your lives. You men are real heroes. Everyone there with you, everyone in the country, is depending on you." It was the director they hardly ever heard from except at Christmas, and every time it was more or less the same shtick. "I'm going to hand things back to Bob and Lou, who will walk you through the endgame. Good luck, men, know that I believe in you, in your training, your professionalism, and that my prayers are with you."

Bob then took the reins. "When you get down to the deck, the reactor core will be to your left and the turbine hall on your right. The heavy water reservoir will be right in front of you under the steam pressure tank. But you will hook up to a bleed valve on the far side of the reactor core and connect the other end of your hose to the reservoir return on the condenser in the turbine hall. That way, we can use the shut-off to draw water to all the units."

Kim understood the strategy immediately even though she was shaking with convulsions in her gut. It made sense to use the water for the moderator instead of coolant water, but then they would have to bypass the reactor core with their hose.

"There's less risk this way"—Lou on the call turned out to be the local fire chief from the entrance to the installation, it seemed hours ago—"since we need a steady flow in the coolant bath and for steam." But that meant walking all the way around the drum of the reactor core and then a long way over into the turbine hall. Lots could go wrong, Kim was thinking, in that lab-rat maze, her training finding focus through the questions shrieking at her. As the elevator hissed to a soft landing, the men pulled a thick hose out of a canvas bag and cradled it over to her like a python digesting in a tree. Being the smallest of them, after all, she was the one for tight spots. Waiting for the elevator door to open, this time it was a desire to hold her granddaughter's hand and walk along the Great Wall of China under a sky as big and blue as the summers back home with the wind blowing hard, as endlessly hard as drummers calling everyone to the fields, that pushed her out the door. A cresting wave of heat buried her in a dune of sand as soon as she stepped out of the elevator pod and the immense reservoir stretched out in front of her as they had said it would. She could make out some lights on its far shore bobbing and shimmering. Steam was rising in misting curtains from its surface and the dark heavy water roiled in a slow boil. Beyond the massive zeppelin of the boiler tank tethered to its bed by great snaking arcs of pipes, high above the reservoir, lightning sparked and sizzled in the long shadows of the containment vault. Looking out into the dark, flashing emptiness, she thought she saw in one bright, explosive strike a reflection of Fort Jasper at night her tools with the careful gentleness of a dentist digging for a molar, she was lifted by the desire to sit on her grandmother's lap. She remembered her sitting with her friends in the wood panelled basement of someone's house. There was a big group of treaty people over preparing for a demonstration against the new enclosures and clearings the next day. Her grandmother and her friends were sorting out the logistics of the speakers, the police, the food, and the child care, and she was on the floor drawn to her by her warmth, the smell of her soap, and the shiny jewellery she was wearing, big and heavy as the tools now in her hands, wanting her grandmother to pick her up and carry her forever. She tightened the last three bolts and turned the settings to standby and immediately felt the pressure in the room—or was it just her chest?—skyrocket. The emergency lighting briefly dipped and then the background din waffled and she was startled to see two small red flowers blossom on her chest. She got up, looked herself over and all around her, suddenly feeling very cold. One of the reactor staff, high above her on a walkway, seemed to be looking at her, but he or she or they were leaning on the railing and didn't move. So far so good, she said to herself as the system stabilized. So, she gathered up her things, hoisted the heavy hose pack on her shoulder, and started her trek toward the turbine hall, unfolding and trailing the hose as she went. She made her way down a long corridor, over a small bridge, and crawled under a trestle of pipes, rounded two sheds, and sighed. It was a dead end. There was a small ladder going up the side of the shed to its roof. It was a long shot and the hose now felt extremely heavy, so she turned around to go back, and froze. Her goggles flashed red, and when they cleared, she saw a marshmallow standing in the passageway at the far end between the sheds.

An emergency light cycling on a rooftop somewhere caught its helmet, making it blink like a camera flash about to go off. The face under the hood was not exactly featureless but scabbed-over flesh, scarred where its eyes, nose, and mouth used to be. Again she was stabbed by the cold and two small red flowers bloomed on her chest. Her heart was racing and she dropped the hose and ran for the ladder, clambered up and went over onto the roof of the shed. She ran along its length, looking for the elevator pod, seeing more of the white spacesuits moving toward the sheds along gangways and down ladders. At the edge of the roof she climbed down and ran along a long corridor and came to a turn that made her pause.

She was trying to remember which way to turn when red flowers appeared swarming on the walls of the shed to her right, so she turned left and ran. At the end of this corridor there were several doors into the sheds, and one was ajar. She went in and the room was pitch-dark. She bumped into what felt like a desk and leaned on it, trying to get her bearings and visualize her route to the elevator. But the room hived into red flowers swarming all around her, so she jumped on the desk and threw herself through the window out of the shed, somersaulting onto the floor to gather herself into a full sprint down the corridor. Now the flowers were blooming everywhere, and this time she rolled under another array of pipes and found herself back out on the deck. At its far end she could see the elevator pod. She was gasping for breath, in pain everywhere, exhausted, and the distance felt impossible, but she ran hard. The men had pulled out camp chairs and were sitting outside the pod. They had a barbecue going. Four of them got up to urinate into a large glass flask together. One of them saw her running toward them and they

Lue Palmer

WATA TIKA DAN BLOOD

"He come to sin on Sunday. He running from one woman's house, and breaking heads wherever he go. Wicked," say the first, Winsome.

"Ooooh is wicked!" say the second, Hyacinthe, squat up on a rock with her bare leg ankle deep. Her toes under the water that tickle her calf when it splash, wet skirt hoist up in their laps. They reaching into the water and pulling out of it.

At the soul river, down in the water, where spirit float in pools of wet cloth; weaving bloated and swaying. Souls floating like jellyfish around each other. They colour red. They colour blue, black, brown, green, purple. They fold in on themself, floating up like they ready for the judgment day.

"Well Iiii say he not long for the world. Long time pass we decide what fi do with him," say the third, Merle. She was not amused—always concern with comings and goings, rights and wrongs.

"Wickedness, it come and go. No saying when or why," say Winsome, reaching into the water and pulling out the soul cloths.

They spread the cloth out and lay them flat. Their wrinkled hands running across them, feeling the fibres. They listening, listening for song and greeting—the threads of each soul chatting out the tune of a lifetime.

Hyacinthe reach into the water and pull out a soul cloth. It small. The thread run short, the weaving cut off before the bottom sew up. She spread it out and look it over. Winsome and Merle leaning to look at the pickney soul, laying with the water soak up. Hyacinthe look at him life, hanging in the short thread. She read him story sad. She breathe heavy and put him back in the water.

"We pray next time him fate be kinder," Hyacinthe say. They put him soul cloth in the water, and send him gently down the river bend.

Many they put back in the water, bless them and push them down the river. But others they ring them quick like a snap neck, like pulling the colour from the cloth throat. They feed them to the water, sink them down where the riverbed swallow them whole. And the river bottom hungry today.

Some soul they fuss and fight on.

"This woman never have a kind word for no one," say Winsome. "The only time she talk to she neighbours when she have gossip!"

"If gossip a sin then we ought to throw you down the river bottom with her!" say Hyacinthe. They fussing and fighting. Hyacinthe snatch the cloth up and push it rough down the river. She grab a stick and jook it round the bend.

Merle sit down pon the rock. She drag up a cloth from the water. It light blue. She sweep it up and naked it come. She look it real close. She poke her tongue out and she taste it. She press it to her face the same way she tilt a cheek to the sun. She hold it close to her chest and rock it from side to side.

Hyacinthe and Winsome crane their necks. "Merle, who that you got there?"

Merle press her lips tight. "Nobody!"

"There's no one so important as a nobody," Hyacinthe call back.

Winsome reach over and drag up the blue cloth and lay him out across the stone. The thread criss and cross. Some part shine in the sun, some part rip and ragged. She spread him out end to end, stretched flat and wide. And the soul lay quivering in the cool breeze.

The three look down upon him. Merle hand twist in her lap as they look at him—her baby boy come to meet he judgment time.

"Get on with it," they say. Merle begin slow, reading the soul threads, for the story of her son spread out naked across the stone.

"Huncle he was a sweet boy," she begin. "He like sorrel juice, and Christmas dinner, cool breeze, and riding he bike in the summertime."

She stop, and Winsome continue.

"An he grew to be a sweetman, they say. Someone who can hear the coo of a young woman sigh, and know just where to touch her waist, know just how to wring her wrist, and just how to eye her thigh and fatness to make her walk quick—make her head lower and speak hush."

"He knew a lot about cover curtain and roll down car window and swimming pool corner. He knew what kinda sweet juice look tasty in the summer and how to spend a dime on a girl and get back a dollar's worth.

"Huncle lived in three places: number thirty-six apartment

with the clean lawn, sat up by the grand cemetery on the pothole road; on the street corner by the Second Drink, the bar where everybody outside yelling and swaying out the loud nighttime; and in the soft part up a woman leg-back, in the round wet pupils with dark holes, the hollow parts of her chest that beat quick at the look of snakes coming through the grass—

"Huncle was a diplomat, a quick pool player, a gardener and a Sunday school teacher; a Saturday's child, the sixth of seven children, an uncle to ten pickney, a lover to three women; a clean-hand man with no dirt under his nails, so he say."

Merle run a shaking finger down the thread, where it catch and rip, a ragged hole in the fabric. And Winsome go on reading it:

"Come Christmas dinner, a likkle pickney dash herself behind window curtain, with belly full of pudding and cakes, sticky fruit fingers running down lace, eyes thick with up-past-bedtime. Behind the window curtain. And this is where she get caught. Huncle, clean-hand man, who like nothing better than a fully belly girl."

Merle stagger back, her leg splash in the water and her body gone stiff. She fall back and they catch her. Her eye roll and she wail and cry. She wail out to the sky.

What she do to deserve such a son? Such a man as this? Her baby boy come to meet he judgment time.

Merle hand shake and she reach out to him. Naked soul spread out across the rock. She hold the twisted thread in her hand, fresh and wet like the first day he born. Her mouth gone dry as she look to him.

"Wickedness. It come and it go. No saying when or why," she say slow.

And then she wring him quick like a snap neck.

Michelle Porter

LUCK IS A LADY

Her first thought was that the flashing lights meant her street would be cleared and salted by morning, that she'd been lucky and wouldn't have to risk death just to drive off the bloody hill their rental had been built on, halfway up and halfway down.

From her bed she watched as the light burst around her curtains in flashes and she let a rare feeling of relief wash over her entire body, until it came to her that she hadn't moved the car the night before. She sat up in a panic and groped for a sweater to pull over her pajamas. She couldn't afford to have her car towed, couldn't pay the fine and groceries both, couldn't pay for all the cabs she'd have to use. She let out a string of profanities in what she knew was her outdoor voice, but her husband, who was sleeping the sleep of a man on painkillers, did not wake to tell her to calm down. She was too groggy to be quick, so she was still struggling with the second sock when the room flooded with light again and there was a sudden blare of a siren. It was just a quick blast, but it was enough to let her know that there were no snowplows out there. Then the sock just slipped over her foot, no problem.

The room flared up again as another cop car pulled onto the street and in the light she noticed a nest of dark hair on her pillow. She'd been doing that again, pulling her hair out as she slept. Although she didn't really sleep anymore. Doctor had offered pills, but with her husband medicated all the time now, someone had to be able to wake up at night for the kids.

And even then, sitting on the edge of the bed, she found one of her hands at the hair at the nape of her neck, pulling. Another beam of light splashed into the room without knocking or asking permission and she stood up. From the window she arranged her hair in a braid and watched as two officers pursued a man down a snowy path between the houses. Seemed like this happened every couple of nights now, ever since that single mom and her kids moved out of the little house beside theirs and some drug operation moved in. They all disappeared into the thickly falling snow, but she knew where the chase would end: drifts as high as their waists, discarded needles, and frozen piles of dog shit.

On the bed her husband shifted. She dropped the curtain and left the room because she knew that, if he woke now, they would wrestle their way into an argument.

Downstairs. Fill the kettle and put it on the stove to boil. Briefly hold the broken electric kettle over the open garbage bin only to return it to the counter because her husband insisted he was going to get it working again, not that she believed him. Take an ibuprofen to make the headache and the coming day a little easier to bear. Set herself down in a chair to wait for the water, surrendering to the solitude.

Of course, her daughter cried out and there she'd gone and hit the table with her palm and swore like a sailor. Even as she told herself she wouldn't go, that the child needed to sleep through one night in her stupid life, she was on her way up the stairs. There was Mandy on the floor beside her big-girl bed crying in small gasps. She put her hand on the girl's back and said something to the child but who knows what. She took a quick look at Mandy's younger brother, who was still sleeping thank God, and lifted Mandy into her bed. Her hands met with wet pajamas and wet sheets. She groaned. She would have to change the sheet and that would probably wake Jason and then she'd have to get them both to sleep all over again.

It's no use to hate the child, she thought.

Even in the darkness she could see the sparkles twinkling from her daughter's homemade Advent calendar. It was tacked to the wall beside the bed. Downstairs the kettle boiled and the shrill whistle pierced the darkness.

Just so you know, her panic over the car being towed wasn't only because of the fines. It was because of what she'd left in the trunk two days ago, left to freeze. It'd be just her luck, she thought, if she'd been found out. Not that it was a big deal, really. And how would they know even if they'd towed her car and looked in the goddamn trunk? They wouldn't think anything of it.

Two days ago and there she'd been in the car they wouldn't be able to afford come January, delivering food to the needy. Way back in September she'd had a rare burst of energy and decided it would be a good idea to volunteer. At the time, Jack'd had a job interview and they'd been sure his injuries would heal up quick, but one fall down a slick front porch and come December she was hauling boxes in the back of her car gassing up ten bucks at a time and wondering how they'd pay their heat bill.

Turning off Long's Hill that day, she was thinking about her husband saying to the kids that it'd be good for them to learn to live on less. He'd grown up, as he said, around the bay, and he was used to doing without. She wasn't from anywhere really, though she said Winnipeg if anyone asked. Only family of hers that Jack knew about was the one sister, whose occasional phone call usually led to more sleepless nights. Sure, they could move in with one of his older brothers if need be, sure babe, there was an extra room. Jack said his luck had run right out, sure, but that it'd come right on back to him one day. Jack said a lot of stuff, didn't he.

She was tired. Her head was itchy from the hairnet she'd been wearing all day. Didn't want to talk to anybody either, not after "can I help you" and "have a nice day" had crossed her tongue at least a thousand times.

On Livingstone Street now, just down the hill a bit from their place. Christmas lights on display here. She'd checked her list on her phone before she started driving, but she couldn't remember the first name of the man she was delivering to, only that his last name was Murphy, same as hers. What was his first name? God, her memory was shot these days. She parked along the road, turned off the engine, and popped the trunk. She caught her own reflection in the rear-view mirror. Her hairline had been picked away and when she tried to pull her hair into something nearing presentable, a clump came out in her hands.

Well, better get a move on if she was going to pick up Jack and the kids on time. Jack had got the kids all excited about buying her a Christmas present. She didn't like the idea, but he'd promised he'd use his walker and to call if it got to be too much. The kids promised to stay right by dad's side and not to run off. And Jack promised not to spend any real money on the goddamn gift.

She parked the car in front of the house. She sat a moment and thought how it wasn't only them having hard times, not if this Murphy guy and the others were on the list to get a food hamper. She got out of the car and picked her way over the ice to the trunk. And there was his box, filled with tinned stew and soup, cans of kidney beans and tomatoes. There were small boxes of macaroni and two different kinds of cookies. There was a loaf of bread and cheese slices, condensed milk and a litre of fresh milk. And, oddly, a complete gingerbread house kit.

Was this Murphy guy going to put that house together? She imagined Mandy and Jason being excited about making a gingerbread house and then she just took the kit out of Murphy's box and tucked it in the back of her trunk. It'll be as if it fell out by accident, she thought. She stood a moment longer and yanked at her hair a couple of times before she reached for the package of processed cheese slices, thinking her kids would love to have them in their sandwiches, thinking of her husband, who was eating bread and margarine most days now.

Okay, she thought, so two things fell out, that's normal. What about the tea? They were almost out of tea. So, another thing fell out. Not a big deal. She lifted the box, closed the trunk, and walked carefully up the walkway to the Murphy guy's affordable housing unit. He must have been watching, because the porch light turned on and the door opened before she was up the steps. A surge of panic tightened her chest. Had he seen her take things out of the box? In the flush of yellow light she could see a skinny old man squinting at her, sizing her up. Snow was falling then, wet and grey like rain.

Come on, come on, he said.

She barely nodded at the old man and walked in.

There was no way he could have seen into the trunk, she told herself. She dropped the box on a counter and said she was going back for the turkey. Back out at the car, she looked at the things that'd fallen out of the box—okay, the things she'd taken. She only wished she had the guts to steal a turkey. But she was never brave enough, not with the important things.

After she dropped the frozen bird on the counter, the old man grabbed her arm and whispered, I have a secret.

What? she said.

He said, You know, I don't really need your boxes.

She shivered. She thought of what she'd left on the bottom of her trunk. Thought how stupid she was not to take more, how she was always a coward, too timid.

His breath was sour and his hand was sweaty and hot. In fact the little townhouse was quite warm. He probably didn't have to pay his own heat, she thought. She repeated the phrase that was her line for these deliveries. She said, We can all use a little help. Glancing around the small kitchen, she noted holes in the plastic tablecloth, the chipped coffee mug, and the stained linoleum floor. She could hear the television playing a commercial from the living room.

I have something coming my way, he said.

That's nice, she said. She pulled her arm from his hand and moved toward the front door.

I'll show you, he said with a slight whine in his voice. Then he paused and added, For a kiss, I will.

He was quick. He wrapped his fingers around her wrist and leaned in. She went completely, stupidly still, the way she did in situations like these, and he pressed his lips against hers. He tasted of warm beer. The smell of him made her want to crawl out of her skin. It lasted barely a moment and then he was pulling her over to a brown side table. She felt a trickle of sweat drip from her scalp. He pulled open a small drawer.

Look here, he said.

He lifted out a child's notebook and flipped through its pages until he found what he was looking for.

See, he said.

She looked at the book. Tucked between two empty pages was a lottery ticket.

You see that? It's mine, he crowed.

He flipped it over. He'd signed the back, *M. Murphy*.

What was his first name? For the life of her, she couldn't remember. She nodded her head. She took a step away and glanced through the kitchen to the front door.

He picked up the ticket and held it inches from her face. It's a winner, he said. What do you think now? Eh? Never guessed that, did you?

He followed her to the kitchen. Don't believe me?

She started to say something, anything really, but he interrupted.

Let me show you this, then, he said.

He shuffled into the living room and returned holding a small piece of torn paper. Damned unreasonable panic. She sucked in a slow breath to calm herself. He put the piece of paper on the table.

I wrote these numbers down at the store, he said. I didn't believe it either when I saw the draw on the TV, so I went over to the store to write down the numbers. There. There's your proof!

He hit a fist against the table for emphasis. The sound frightened her and she couldn't stop herself jumping away. He looked at her, a sly grin on his face. You the type that startle easy, eh? My wife was like that. Spooked easy she did.

She looked at the numbers. Congratulations, she said.

His old face lit up. He said, I'm saving it for when my daughter comes to visit, if she comes. She promised she'd come after the New Year. What a surprise that'll be for her, eh? What do you think?

What did she think? She thought he needed to pretend he was better than he was. She thought he needed a story to keep him warm sitting in this place all alone all day and all night. She thought he was pretty far gone and that he believed his own delusions. She'd seen old men like this before.

She offered a nod for an answer. Satisfied, he took his paper and left the kitchen.

She put her hand on the table to steady herself.

Well, she called out, got another delivery. Good luck, you know, with your daughter and everything. Merry Christmas.

What? Oh yeah. Christmas to you too.

He was busy putting the notebook away. She took a package of cookies from the box on the counter and dropped them in the trunk before she drove away.

One more delivery and then up to the mall to get her husband. He'd texted for her to park and come help with the kids, so she parked, and when she found them sitting in the food court, they were full of their secret. Mandy couldn't help herself, said, I promised not to tell, Mommy, but it's going to look so pretty in your hair. Jack shushed her and said, Don't worry, I didn't spend a crazy amount. She knew immediately that he'd spent more than they could afford, damn him.

She agreed to let the kids share one doughnut and then everyone stopped near the rear doors to get their coats on. A woman holding a clipboard caught her eye and approached. Mandy and

Jason began to bicker the moment the woman started to talk. I'm asking people to sign my petition, she said. Jack told Jason to get his coat on and she wrangled with Mandy. We're demanding rights for this country's agricultural workers, the woman said. Because our cheap food is bought on the backs of their underpaid labour.

Get your coat on, Jack said again.

Jason was knocking his body against Mandy so that she couldn't get her arm into her sleeve. The woman asked if she cared about the human rights of migrant workers and would she sign the petition? Jason butted Mandy again.

Fucking stop it, she snapped, and she gave him a shove to get him out of the way. She'd pushed a lot harder than she meant to. He fell over, started screaming. The woman with the petition glared. People nearby whispered. The look Jack gave her, watchful and hurt. He called to Jason, who ran to him, and then he said, I think Mommy needs time alone today. Jason clung to his daddy's leg.

Back home, she brought the walker into the house, but left all the stuff that had fallen from the Murphy guy's box in the trunk.

Later, after dinner, she said to Jack that they'd have to take Mandy out of swimming lessons. Just the way it was. They'd been in the kitchen. It'd been dark for hours. The kids were already asleep. That look on Jack's face. She could tell the pain was pretty bad. He didn't look at her, didn't say nothing to her. Reached for the filmy yellow bottle, swallowed two blue pills with a sip of water. Left. She followed him to the hallway.

Talking to you is useless, she spat at him.

He shook his head, went upstairs to sleep. He could do things like that, sleep in the middle of a storm, after a fight, when babies cried, when others needed him.

Oh, this was one of those winter storms that began slow as fat snowflakes then reinvented itself in a wet fury, crashing against the house, worrying the windows. Kids asleep again, bed dry. Police cars gone now too. She was alone in the kitchen again, listening to the coming and going of cars and people, thinking how it had all become part of the musical score of her life: rumbling car engines; incessant footsteps up and down the dealer's stairs; the slamming of the doors. She herself provided the high notes of worry and the painfully taut violin strings. Sleep was the maddened conductor, a driven, unsatisfied master.

Such a pounding in her head now. Damned ibuprofen didn't work. Her hair no longer in its braid and she kept reaching and pulling, reaching and pulling. Kept thinking about that Murphy guy. About what was in the trunk of her car. The electric heater creaked hot, but she was cold. She put her head down on the table for a moment of rest.

She woke to find herself standing in her coat and boots outside her house. She couldn't remember how she'd come to be there. Hair caught in a sloppy ponytail, too matted for a braid. Icy rain tormenting her face, pestering every piece of bare skin. She felt a shopping bag in her hand. It came to her that she'd been to the trunk and that she was returning things. Down the hill. Down the hill.

Had he been waiting for her? The door opened a sliver after one knock. When he recognized her face, he pulled the door open wider, muttered, Come in out of the weather, love. He must be a fellow insomniac, she thought.

She offered no explanation for showing up in the darkness of the night, in the fury of a storm. He only asked if she wanted a drink. He wore a robe, faded and unwashed. He put a hand on her shoulder, pressed near. She put the bag on his counter.

Yes, a drink would be nice, she said.

She left him to sort out the bottle opener and mug, walked out of the kitchen and right to the side table drawer. The notebook was there, pushed right to the back. Inside the notebook was the ticket. She lifted it, held it between thumb and finger. She took out her phone, checked the numbers.

He brought a mug of beer over as she was putting her phone back in her pocket. He saw the wide-open notebook and the ticket. Even slightly drunk he knew what was happening.

He bellowed in outrage. He threw the mug at her. It hit her in the chest and that one act seemed to rip away the cloak of passivity with which she had been living all her life. She gasped. Then he was upon her, scratching and pawing. He was an old wolf, desperate to keep his place. He had not anticipated a challenge from an animal like her.

They fell to the ground, each groping for the other's arms, trying to pin the other down. It was almost like lovemaking, and this recognition sharpened her senses even more.

No, it is not difficult to kill him. It is not difficult to hold him down, to cover his mouth, and to block his nose. It is easy.

It is, she thinks, as he struggles and twitches as if in orgasm, like killing myself. There is a sense of accomplishment for this thing she has done. But once she is done, once the ticket is in her hand, she can face neither the active, vigorous body nor the inert, dead house he had been living in.

She's thinking enough to take the bag of fallen items with her. She pulls her coat sleeves over her hands to avoid touching anything, the walls, the door handles. Once she has opened the door, she discovers she can't close it again. She's so out of breath she has to stop to rest on the steps leading back up the hill to her house. She's never had to do this before. She empties the contents of her stomach on the street and watches while the torrents of rain wash it downhill. Soon there is a nearly imperceptible shift in the quality of light, the coming of morning. She is soaked through but feels lighter, able to go on.

At home, Jack is snoring. The ticket, the ticket. Does she have it? Panic. Oh yes, yes. She does. She adds Jack's name to the signature line. She underlines *M. Murphy,* her first initial and her last name, and then folds the precious ticket carefully into Jack's wallet. She hesitates over the old ticket still in his wallet. Would it be better to take it out? It doesn't matter either way, she decides, and leaves it. She returns the wallet to the side pocket of his winter coat.

Everything is going to be okay, she says to the wallet, to the jacket, to the house, and most of all to Jack.

Shower. She does not feel clean. Her hair is ungovernable, too many tangles that she'll never work through. There are tiny scissors in the first aid kit. She uses these to cut away all her hair, right down to an inch from her scalp. Clumps collect in the bottom of the tub and form a scummy plug. The water is rising. First covering her toes, then her heels, now the bottom of her shins.

She hears her daughter calling. Shuts off water. She steps out, towels herself until her skin is pink. Mandy yells louder. She hurries, does not want Jack to wake yet. She is sitting on the edge of Mandy's bed now, in the dark. She is holding her child, whispering, Everything is going to be okay. Just that one sentence, over and over.

Mandy sucks her thumb and studies her mother. She reaches out and strokes her mother's fuzzy new hair. When her mother forgets to speak, whenever she ceases the repetition of the verse, the child demands more. Say it again, Mama. Again. When Jack woke, they were still there, just like that. He navigated his way to the bathroom on a pair of crutches. Mother and child fell silent, listening to his morning noises. When he came out again, she called out, Jack? When you've a minute, check our lottery ticket, would you?

He stopped in the doorway of the kids' bedroom. The hallway light shone around him. He couldn't really see them in the shadows, but he offered a sort-of-smile, half affection, half apology. Never stop hoping, do ya? He turned, walked away. Called back, But coffee first. Never disappoint a person before coffee, that's what I say. She listened to his slow navigation of the stairs, heavy and awkward. Heard coffee-making noises in the kitchen. Scoot over a bit, she told Mandy. The child did. She rolled under the blankets and together they lay in bed, breathing in each other's smell. What was that he was singing? Was it "Luck Be a Lady"? She pressed her face into the blankets to hold back a laugh.

How many days before Christmas now, Mama?

Oh, I don't know. Let me count, sweetie, she said.

How many?

I think it's six, my girl, she said. Six days before Christmas.

She could wait.

Even if it took the whole fucking morning for Jack to make the coffee.

Sara Power

///////////////

THE CIRCULAR MOTION
OF A PROFESSIONAL
SPIT-SHINER

Joyce is practising her tightrope mime routine. Suppresses her bounce with a tilt of her pelvis as she lifts her right foot to advance on the tightrope. There is no rope, of course. The sound of a bagpipe practice chanter seeps through the dormitory walls. Roy is practising his scales.

A care package from her dad arrived last week. *Love Dad,* the card says. *Congrats! You made it through first year, xoxo.* Oreos, Oh Henry! bars, Skittles. His scratchy handwriting makes Joyce pang for home and she opens a package of Oreos. Sitting at her desk, she flips through her college handbook, pausing on a vintage photograph of The Old 18—the first eighteen gentlemen cadets to enter the Royal Military College in 1876. In the photograph, the gentlemen cadets wear pillbox hats with black chinstraps indenting their cheeks, scarlet doeskin tunics embroidered in gold, brass buttons descending their fronts. Like wind instruments, she thinks, as she eats another cookie whole. The gentlemen cadets' uniforms are identical to the one she'll wear on graduation parade in two weeks. It still doesn't feel real to her.

Last August, when she first entered her quarters in the Lasalle building, it struck her how plain the interior was compared with the Tudor entranceway and the parapeted side gables and buttresses of the exterior. She had imagined ornate ceilings and stairwells, but the interior was more echo chamber than Gothic collegiate. Acoustics absorbed into quadrangles of carpeted hallways and squat rooms. Austere, grey, uniform spaces. The place still feels austere and grey to her, except for Roy. Roy is an infinite source of generosity, she thinks, as he bleats through the opening bars of "Scotland the Brave."

Joyce stands and braces her body to walk across the tightrope. It's not that she has to make herself believe she is on a tightrope; she has to make herself forget the tightrope isn't there. Leaning over her sink, she forces her fingers down her throat, bringing up clods of Oreo, sweet and bitter. She rinses her mouth and washes her hand.

*

The first six weeks at RMC are known as recruit term, a gruelling period of initiation when recruits are under the constant supervision of select third-year cadets. Joyce and Roy stood side by side during daily inspection and she recognized something particular about his scent—something dank and familiar, like the morning scent of a sibling. He had shadowy temples and a concave chest, was incapable of remembering drill commands or historical dates, could barely manage ten push-ups, and limped behind on morning runs. In the evenings, recruits were penalized with *circles* for failing to meet designated standards. Recruit flights formed up on the side of the parade square to watch the underperformers sprint the perimeter. Roy ran circles almost every evening, his skinny legs gangly and puppet-like.

Recruit room layout included hospital-cornered beds, socks rolled into ovals, shirts folded ten inches by ten inches. On the shelf above the sink, a bar of soap, a razor, deodorant, toothpaste, and a toothbrush were aligned and spaced according to the manual. The sink had to be dry; the trash can, empty. Recruit staff arrived at 05h00 to storm the quarters with white gloves and rulers. When Third-Year Nadeau found a red pubic hair on Roy's bar of soap, she held it in front of his face. "Disgusting," she had barked. Part of the inspection layout was a framed photo of a loved one, and Roy displayed his sister, who was an Olympic rower. His nickname became the Olympian.

*

BY THE RIGHT___QUICK___MARCH. It's graduation parade practice and the Cadet Wing Training Officer yells drill commands over the bagpipes. As Joyce marches in file, she feels a fleeting connection to something giant and historic. The precision, the synchronization, the percussive sound of boots on pavement like a collective pulse. First-Year Pellerin is in front of her in file, and she notices his neck, can see the razor burn there. In recruit term, Pellerin joked about how small Third-Year Nadeau's tits were. *She loves cock,* he had whispered to the others. BY THE LEFT___RIGHT___TURN. Pellerin's drill was flawless, and in her peripheral vision, Joyce watches his gait and extends her step to match. She imagines a board connecting the base of her skull to her tailbone, a technique she acquired in mime that works in situations which demand both rigidity and flexion.

It was Roy who introduced Joyce to mime back in October. During their first free weekend after recruit term, dressed in their navy-blue, #4 uniforms, they marched off the college grounds, saluting the Memorial Arch as they passed.

TRUTH DUTY VALOUR

Blow out your bugles over the rich dead
There's none of these so lonely and poor of old
But dying has made us rarer gifts than gold.

Princess Street shops were bustling, and Joyce had a sharp sense of her surroundings. It was her first time being in uniform in public, and it might have been another dimension. Never in her life had she felt so seen; she paid close attention to her posture.

They entered a café on Brock Street called The Moth and found themselves in the middle of a mime open-mic. When seated, they ordered two towering pieces of raspberry cheesecake.

Joyce liked the silent mode of suggestion offered in mime. Instead of commands and orders and the forcing of will, mime asked for understanding in a playful, malleable way. After the third or fourth act, Roy walked to the stage and performed a short skit, miming a waiter in a diner, getting hoots of laughter when he whipped imaginary customers with an imaginary dishcloth.

It was the first time she threw up her food, and the emptying left her with a sense of satisfaction. A sense of an altered self— not a self that might fit into this military life she had chosen, but one that could release her from time to time—a self she could control in this elemental way.

Joyce and Roy are polishing their parade boots together in the cadet common room with her dad's care package between them on the floor.

"Take one," she says, throwing an Oh Henry! bar at him. "Take them all, please."

"My parents and sister arrive tomorrow," he says, taking a chocolate bar.

"The Olympian!"

"Sherri doesn't compete anymore," Roy says. "She retired after Atlanta. Her body couldn't take it." His mouth yawns open as he breathes on the toe of his boot, readjusting the yellow Kiwi cloth around his pointer and middle fingers, polishing in small circles the way Joyce had shown him. "So, did you hear about Fourth-Year Gibbs?"

Joyce shakes her head, eating Skittles one by one.

"He fell!" Roy says with a grin. "He fell on parade today. Hungover apparently. Sliced his hand with his bayonet."

Joyce squirrels her own hand inside her boot and holds it up, the glassy shine like the black of a lake. Her face stares back, disproportioned and creaturely.

"Karma," Roy says. "I still think you should report the fucker."

Joyce packs up her stuff to leave. "I'm goin' for a run."

"Sorry . . . don't go, Joyce! It's after ten, for God's sake. I'm sorry to bring it up."

Outside, Joyce takes off at a clip past the adjacent dormitories of Lasalle and Haldimand. There's a hint of fresh paint from the bleachers on the inner field, and she runs past the stone wall of Fort Frederick and cuts across the grass to the St Lawrence River. Lights of Kingston reflect on the water and the Wolfe Island ferry is docking. She can hear the drone of a vehicle as it crosses the Kingston bridge. Gibbs, she thinks, imagining his sliced hand.

*

Every year in October, the end of recruit term is celebrated with a college-wide party where beer is sold by the pitcher. Within the first hour, most cadets have removed their beer-soaked shirts. After six weeks of no eye contact with anyone outside her recruit flight, Joyce was met with an entirely new set of faces. There were only a handful of first-year girls, and everyone knew who she was. She felt the eyes on her. It was exhilarating.

On the dance floor, a tall, lean, shirtless guy grabbed her wrist, smiling. Another cadet with his shirt wrapped around his head grabbed her other wrist. They pressed in close, and she danced between them. The first guy looked down at Joyce's body attentively, examining her. He linked his hands around her lower back and moved loosely with the music, closing his eyes, as if entering a fantasy that had nothing to do with her. She liked it. She liked his vacuous state, his bitter, musky scent. The second guy was behind her, in sync, the three of them folding into one another, reciprocating.

It was when they were joined by Fourth-Year Gibbs that the harmony was disrupted. A crude #9 painted on his chest, Gibbs wedged himself between them. The first guy stiffened, but continued to dance as Gibbs wrapped his shirt around Joyce's neck. He was playful, shimmying into her as he manoeuvred the shirt down her back. Then, abruptly, he tied the shirt around her head. He tied it so tightly her earrings cut into her neck. She was blindfolded. She tried to wrestle the shirt from her face, but it wouldn't come off. Bodies closed in around her. Hands mauled her stomach, her armpits. Fingers pressed and prodded between her legs. She pulled and pawed at the blindfold as hands grabbed her breasts and a hard cock pressed into her back. Lashing out, she flailed, smacking at the bodies that surrounded her as a pitcher of cold beer was dumped over her head.

Joyce bit down hard on her tongue and lost her balance, falling into a greasy, slick chest, then to the floor. On the floor, she tugged at the blindfold until it released. Her head was spinning, the skin on her face was raw, and around her, a small circle of shirtless guys was uncurious as they backed away. She walked off the dance floor and the circle that had formed closed in and disappeared.

*

Joyce picks up her pace as she sprints around Point Frederick Drive, the taste of Skittles on the roof of her mouth. The Wolfe Island ferry is making its way to the island now. Back at Fort Frederick, she opens the large wooden door and enters, where the giant belly of a Martello tower looms over grassy banks that form an arrowhead. Barrels of gunpowder were once stored within these earthworks, and after the recruit obstacle course, she and the other members of her flight had stood in single file inside the dark, musty tunnels, taking turns drinking some unknown sludge, reciting one by one, a quote from the college's first Commandant:

Valour, gentlemen as the heritage of the grand old stock from which we are all sprung. If you are true, if duty is your star, you are sure to be brave.
Truth Duty Valour

Her face is sweating. One hand on her knee, she roots her fingers down her throat, emptying herself of Skittles.

*

On the Sunday before graduation parade, Joyce and Roy attend their final open-mic at The Moth before heading off for summer training—Joyce to Gagetown and Roy to Esquimalt. They settle into a nest of mismatched throw pillows in a corner booth. Burgundy velvet drapes graze the floor, and shelves with leather-bound books and vintage cameras create a cozy, clichéd atmosphere. The small stage glows beneath ceiling spotlights, and beers and cheesecake arrive at their table. Roy is practising his skit, shifting his face between expressions of ecstasy, horror, joy, and exhaustion.

"The Mask Maker," he says, gleefully. "A legendary act, the Mask Maker flips masks on and off his face." Roy makes faces, raising his long fingers in peekaboo to switch between each imaginary mask.

"The pathos!" Joyce exclaims.

"Oh, but in the end," Roy continues, "the Mask Maker puts on a laughing face. A terrific laughing face." Roy raises his hands to his face. When he lowers them, his mouth gapes in a broad, gaudy grin. He bounces about in his seat, luxuriating in the joy of his happy face, but as he tries to remove the laughing mask, it won't come off. The mask is stuck! He lowers his shoulders, bows his head, bangs his fist on the table, descends into despair, all the while maintaining the gaping grin on his face.

"Horrific," Joyce mumbles through a mouthful of cheesecake.

"Awesome, right?!" Roy says. "Here's to next year! No Gibbs." He raises his beer and takes a drink.

"He'll bring his tsunami self to Petawawa," Joyce says bitterly. "1RCR apparently."

"Such a dick," Roy says.

"Anyway, you're right. I should report his ass," Joyce says. "I will at some point, maybe." She stares above her at an octopus of a chandelier.

When it's her turn to perform, Joyce walks to the stage, and raises her left arm to catch a hula hoop. She rotates it around her arm, walking rigidly with pointed toes. On stage, she flicks the hoop straight up and catches it on her neck. Bracing her lower body, she maintains the motion of the hoop, her face a triumphant grin. Her eyes shift and fix on something in the middle distance as another hoop darts in her direction. She moves with quick, short steps to catch it with her head and adjusts the rhythm of her circular motion, extending her arms out front, palms up—*ta-da!* Another hoop is tossed, and she locks it in her gaze, scoops her head to catch it. The hoops are out of sync now, but she keeps them moving with violent circles of her head and neck. They slink to her hips and continue frantic laps of her body. Arms out, palms up—*ta-da!* But there is another hoop, and another, and another, and Joyce's spiralling motion deteriorates into jolted, rigid gestures as the hoops continue to descend upon her. Her arms are no longer presenting, but reaching upward desperately, hooking each new hoop as it wraps and flails around her body. She keeps circling and circling and circling, the motion concentrated in her waist, her feet stepping one-two-one-two-one-two-one-two as the hoops continue their orbit around her core. Finally, abruptly, she lowers both arms and catches the hoops.

There are no hoops, of course, but Joyce has faith that her audience can see what is invisible. She bows. She bows deeply to bountiful applause.

Ryan Turner

Ryan Turner

///////////

GHOSTS

At the airport I make my way through security, ascend the escalator to Departures, buy a coffee, and drop into an uncomfortable wooden chair. A spectral light stretches from the bank of windows, and for a time I fall into a peaceful trance, watching all types of people pass, some leisurely and others making a beeline, speeding into the oncoming lane of pedestrians before periodically merging back into regular traffic. It isn't long, however, before I begin to shift and fidget. I am dehydrated and can feel a headache building at the corners of my eyes. As of late, airports upset my stomach and my equilibrium. If I try to read, I feel nauseous. If I don't drink copious amounts of water, my headache worsens, and if I do, I then need to go to the washroom the moment I find myself crammed into the cabin of the plane. I close my eyes and sip my burnt coffee. My jaw feels tender. There's that too—bruxism. Until a few years ago, I was perfectly healthy, and then like an avalanche this new vocabulary of ailments came crashing over me.

"My God, Mark?"

Looking up, I find a lithe, grinning, faintly familiar woman in a black blazer abandoning her suitcase and edging between the tables and chairs towards me. I recognize her with a little leap of surprise as the sister of one of my best friends growing up.

"It's so good to see you!" she says.

"Here," I say, leaning to remove my messenger bag from the opposite chair.

Her name is Jana. She tells me she's on her way home from a medical conference where she presented a paper, and we determine we're on the same flight to Toronto, from where I will continue on to Vancouver.

A moment later, she has her suitcase and her black travel mug of coffee. I'm flattered by her enthusiasm. As children, we couldn't have spoken more than ten words to one another though we spent countless hours in the same house.

"How are you?" I ask, and she describes how she's been trying to live without any form of plastic.

"Snacks are the hardest," she says. "The kids love crackers and all the boxes come with a plastic sleeve, so I've been baking it all myself. It's nice—they get involved."

She asks about Tara, my sister, who's working in management for a regional insurance broker and has two young children. I tell her about my mother's new life in British Columbia, where I'm headed, and how it feels as if she's become an astronaut, as if after a lifetime of answering phones for the federal government she's been suddenly sent off to terraform Mars.

"She's never even been to British Columbia," I say, "and she's never been with another man, not as far as I know. She met my father when she was just out of high school."

I hesitate asking about Luke, her brother, who apparently got into trouble for selling alcohol to minors a decade ago and who, according to my sister, wears sweat pants in public and yet smiles and asks polite questions whenever she sees him.

"How long are you in BC?" she asks.

"A week."

"And you... are you with someone?"

"I was, but we just broke things off." Eight months have passed and yet I find it hard to speak those words aloud without immediately disappearing inside myself. The same month Emily went through with it, she met someone—perhaps she'd already been seeing him, or planning to see him, before the split. He shares my first name, so whenever she posts anything about the two of them on social media—*Mark and I are off to Denmark!*—it seems unintentionally mocking, as if a display of the life I could have had.

"I'm sorry," she says. "Or maybe not. Should I be sorry? Maybe it's a good thing."

"It is," I say, though without conviction.

She asks about dating, *What's that like?* She says it with the same kind of yearning and trepidation other married friends of mine sometimes do. So I tell her about the two or three women who've treated our first dates like screening sessions for impending fatherhood. Do I have any history of depression in my family? Do I smoke? What are my thoughts on paternity leave?

She laughs and, after a pause, seems to remember something. Her eyes narrow.

"I'm sorry about your dad," she says. "I was so sad when I heard."

I thank her and tell her I was likewise sorry to hear about her mother. I recall afternoons arriving to see Luke, a gang of our friends raucous upstairs while I remained at the kitchen table, happy to chat away with Mrs O'Connor.

"You should come visit," she says. "Come see me in Toronto."

I'm so taken aback by the offer that I announce I'll be passing through again next week.

"You're coming into the city?"

"Well." I'd be there about seven hours, I explain. I booked a terrible flight back. "I get in at midnight—it was all they had at the last minute." This is a lie, but I feel sensitive about the truth, that I took whatever was cheapest. "I've got a friend in Mississauga," I add, to soften the insanity of it. "I'll get a few hours' sleep on his couch."

She keeps reaching up to touch the stud in her ear, and whenever she does, I can't help but notice the hollow of her neck. I recall a phase from adolescence when Jana was suddenly as tall as I was. And from this new perspective she'd grown brazen, teasing me, flirting from the safety of her untouchable position. It wasn't only that she was Luke's sister, but that she was four years younger, a child.

When she asks what I do, I describe the politics of the university where I teach English. I don't mention that the job is sessional, or that I have a second job doing science-themed parties for children on the weekends. I recall a birthday boy with an orange ring of Cheezies residue stretching almost to his ears, all the toys in the loot bags I distribute: a bright-blue plastic helix flyer, a key chain with a string of plastic sun beads, a yellow-and-red plastic spin disc.

After finishing our coffee, we walk to our gate, where we keep on talking—about the part of Toronto where she lives and about anyone from the old days with whom we keep in touch.

When our flight begins to board, she tells me she wishes we could stay a while longer. We even strategize switching seats so we can sit side by side on the plane, but it turns out there's a mother with a newborn next to me and our plan never materializes.

*

I brush my teeth in my mother's washroom. The sink seems low and the water leaks once I shut it off, though the fixtures look straight out of their plastic packaging. Every tile and surface is spotless and gives off the gluey odour of recent installation.

In contrast, I catch sight of myself in the oval mirror, the unkempt beard and tired, sunken eyes. Maybe once a month I look hard at my own reflection and wonder if I've yet crossed the line beyond which, if we were to meet, my dead father wouldn't recognize me—so I'd have to say, "Dad, it's me, Mark."

When I was with Emily, not so long ago, I always thought it would be easy finding someone else. I believed possibilities abounded, and I was blind to the ways in which Emily and I had been building something out of our day-to-day tiffs and trivialities, out of our silences, from a brush of a hand at the sink in the morning or a comforting, invisible awareness in the middle of the night.

"Coffee?" says my mother as I amble, half-asleep, down the hall. "I've put some on for you."

I ask if she wants me to save her some and she shakes her head. "Thanks, but I'm rehydrating."

I heard her up and out the door before seven, and she is still in her jogging attire: black leggings and bright-blue jacket. She has long hair with no longer a hint of blond in it, more white than grey. Even now, after her run, she looks elegant and fashionable. Her silvery toque slouched back, not a hair out of place.

At the table, she's searching through the first of three big boxes I helped her carry from her bedroom closet. She lifts out some shirts and blouses and refolds them neatly.

"You know what I must have thrown out in the move?" she says. "A box of letters from your father."

"You threw them out?"

"Not on purpose."

I tell her how I recently came across a stack he'd written me in my first year away. They were printed on school stationery with a dot matrix where you had to fold and tear the paper's edges. In one, he explained to me how an airport works. He warned me to arrive at least half an hour early and go straight to the gate to give them my bags. It was clear he hadn't flown in a while.

I pass into the sitting room, trying to determine which surface is less inviting, the black leather sofa or the white suede chaise longue.

Here is my mother's new home: a sleek downtown Vancouver condo. She looks small to me with the city luminous beyond the tall glass patio doors. The counter-height kitchen table with its tall, spindly-legged chairs might be a repurposed workbench out of the industrial shop classes my father used to teach.

Douglas rents luxury apartments on the internet. Occasionally, if there is a major event, he even rents out their own place, and he and my mother ferry their belongings to one of his other locations—in Kitsilano or North Vancouver or all the way to Vancouver Island.

Last night, just after I arrived, she took me on a tour of all her favourite places: a little park with a fountain, a hole-in-the-wall coffee shop where she knew each of the chatty, bearded baristas by name. *There is nothing to worry about,* she seemed to be communicating. She is like a hearty vegetable that thrives in any environment.

As if to punctuate this message of survival, later she and Douglas had sex. On my laptop at the high kitchen table I over-heard them, desperate and constrained, starting and then stopping, whispering, starting again at an agonizingly slow pace, believing maybe that if they took their time I wouldn't hear. I thought to get up and sneak into the office with the pullout couch where I was sleeping, but feared making a sound. To take my mind off it, I read articles on the internet—the Anthropo-cene, the protests in Hong Kong. I googled why we scratch when we're itchy. I looked at what were supposed to be surprising photographs of a woman I recognized from movies I watched as a kid. Aimlessly, this led to Street View, to the house I'd grown up in—it had new doors and windows but hadn't changed much except for the car in the driveway—and eventually to the Agric-ola Street row house where Emily had recently moved with the other Mark.

I zoomed in, imagining I might find some hint of her in the unlit windows. She'd liked to sit up in our wide front sill reading or, with the book on her chest, gazing up at the sky.

"I'm happy that you're happy," I say to my mother now as she digs into her second box.

"Oh, I am," she says, waving her hands as if the proof is right there all around us.

She was always involved in community theatre—in acting and making costumes and selling tickets—but she seems more animated now than she ever was back home. Her gestures are grander. Her voice is louder.

"Where are you going to put it?" I ask about the urn she's in search of. Not my father's but her more recent loss, her beloved Jack Russell's.

I can't imagine the little walnut case with Franklyn's photo alongside the clean-lined furniture and muted tones or beneath the five-foot-wide charcoal of what looks like tiny buildings stacked in a colossal and precarious heap.

"Oh, I'm going to scatter them," she says, and hesitates a second, catching my eye with a pained smile, for a moment almost breaking from the steely character she's inhabited before snatching a cream sweater from the pile and refolding it with a few deft movements.

"Did I tell you?" she says. "Douglas is giving me some big gift next Sunday." She sets the sweater back on the top of the pile. "God. I hope it's not a ring."

"No?"

"I told him I'm not doing that. Getting married." She pulls the third box towards her. "I'm not going to be one of these women who's always having to distinguish between her first and second husband. Your father was my husband. Douglas is . . . well, *Douglas.*"

My mother came from an upper-middle-class family and then married a passionate repairman who taught at a vocational school. In my childhood, we vacationed in Bangor, Maine, which my sister and I assumed was a major American city. All the rooms of our house (I can see now) had been long out of fashion—the blue carpets and the linoleum and the yellow Formica countertops, the yellow stove and refrigerator. *We had everything we needed,* my mother sometimes says, though I know how she maxed out the credit cards and, until the creditors came calling, told my father elaborate fictions about the money they owed.

In the glow of a sputnik-looking standing light fixture, I watch her digging into the third and final box.

"Aha!" she says, and holds up the modest wooden urn for me to see. "You know, once the girl at the pharmacy called out for a Mr Russell to pick up his prescription, *I have something here for a Mr Russell,* and when no one else answered, I said, *Well, he's a Jack Russell, so* ... Everyone in line got a kick out of that."

I've heard this story. Sometime in the recent past she began retelling the same stories—not the same two or three (she isn't there yet) but the same two or three dozen. Months might pass before an anecdote comes back around, and at first I told her outright: *Mom, you've already told me this.* But now I realize I've quit acknowledging this repetition. I only half listen. I wonder if this pretending is more cruel or kind. At the same time, this bit of frailty seems proof that the mother I knew is still in there, beneath the shell of pragmatism and self-directed tough love.

"It kind of worked out," she says, meaning Franklyn's death. "It would have been impossible to move out here otherwise."

"Mom."

"What? It's just the truth."

"Well, good. So you made the right choice, then," I say with an edge in my voice. While my sister was supportive of the move, I insisted it was lunacy—selling her house, leaving all her friends and family, taking such violent risks. And for what? Some man she barely knew?

But instead of telling me again how much she loves her new life, she gives me a look I can't quite decode.

"What?" I ask.

She turns to the window, where there's a sad little puff of cotton clouds.

"Let me just say that Douglas cuts some corners," she says. "He has some strange ideas that your father would never approve of."

"What kind of ideas?"

She shrugs and gives me another cryptic look, cocking her neatly manicured brow.

"He's not hurting you?" I feel my stomach lurch.

"Oh, heavens no."

"You don't have to see anything out, Mom. There's no shame in coming home."

She frowns, disappointed in where I've taken this. "I'm fine. I shouldn't have mentioned it. I admit I got caught up in a bit of a whirlwind with Douglas, but maybe I needed to get caught up in something." And with barely a beat, "What about you? Have you met anyone? I think forty is worse than my age. At least I had a crop of widowers."

"Actually," I say, "I met someone on the plane."

"Oh." She sets down the urn. "That's exciting. What's she like?"

"Married," I say, deciding against mentioning that the woman was Jana.

Her face drops. "Too bad."

*

Emily and I were dog-sitting when Franklyn stopped eating. There were nights when I got up and found him standing sheepishly under the kitchen table, his hind legs quivering, a puddle beneath him. Franklyn refused to sleep in the bed with me and Emily the way he used to. He'd gone half-blind and kept running into things. His ear was bloody from one such accident. His hair was matted, his blindness had brought with it an intense fear of water.

For months, my sister and I had been pleading with our mother to put him down, and for a day or two she would concede. She'd book the appointment and call one of us to have a good cry, but just before it was time to follow through, she'd tell me how Franklyn was eating well again and she didn't mind looking after him. She didn't want to be hasty just to unburden herself.

When I took him to the vet in the middle of that week I was looking after him, I swaddled him in a blanket to hide him from view. *He's in pain,* said the vet after a cursory assessment. *He's got a dozen issues and any one of them could be fatal.* Her tone was accusatory and filled me with shame on my mother's behalf. *You need to do the right thing here.* I crouched to meet him at eye level, rubbed his velvety ears back, and kissed the soft crown of his head. Not so long ago, he'd been still energetic, still apt to find me on the sofa and push a tennis ball into my crotch, and I wasn't sure why, but it had been easier to imagine the lifeless body of my father than of this dog I'd known less than half as long. Maybe what made the difference was witnessing the entire life cycle. Ever after it would seem to me that the life of a dog is played in such accelerated motion that all the indignities of ailing joints and clouded eyes are already written in a young dog's body.

Though the vet strongly urged me to *give him peace,* I told her it wasn't my decision to make.

Three days later, I called my mother and sister at a beach resort in Mexico to say we'd lost him.

"Should I tell her?" I asked Tara when she picked up. "Or should I wait?"

"Well, there's nothing she can do."

I waited and called again on the morning they were set to fly home.

"I'm so sorry, Mom. He died Tuesday."

She asked about an autopsy. She wanted to speak with the vet to get the cause of death.

"Just natural causes," I said. "He wasn't in any pain."

"But was it his epilepsy? It couldn't have been cancer. We just got through all those scans."

Franklyn had been staying in Halifax with me and Emily, and the day after I'd consented to have him put down, I'd driven the two hours to my mother's so she wouldn't have to return to a house full of Franklyn's toys.

"What did you do with them?" she asked on the phone from Mexico when I told her about packing away all of Franklyn's effects.

I said they were in a box in the basement.

"Why would you do that?" She insisted it would be worse having the house empty, finding no trace of him, and so I drove back and returned the mangled stuffed sheep to where I'd found it lying in the kitchen. I returned the treat balls and the tennis balls and the dozen bits of chewed bones.

My mother had never lived completely on her own. When my father died, she still had Franklyn, and so after Franklyn's death I worried she'd descend into a dark oblivion—that the death of her dog would actualize the death of her husband.

Instead, she met Douglas, a retired architect, that December. By April she had her house on the market. And over the course of the next few months she'd made the move to British Columbia all the way from New Brunswick—to that Vancouver condo from the large but cluttered two-storey where she'd spent more than thirty years.

After a late lunch with my mother on her high balcony, I retreat to my room at the end of the hall. I check email—a personal account and then one for work. In a rush, I skim the day's tennis scores before moving to the page that's been on my mind for hours. I read a few posts, which aren't Jana's but causes she's championing: a fundraiser for muscular dystrophy, somebody running to raise money for a Toronto school. After navigating to her photos, I hungrily pass through a decade in reverse. There are her three daughters—sleeping, swimming, dressed like Russian dolls for Hallowe'en. As I click, they get younger and vanish, one by one. There is a wedding in San Francisco when Jana is heavily pregnant. A trip to Ireland with her hair cut short and dyed blond. The man in the pictures, whom I assume is her husband, appears to be a sort of versatile carpenter who makes cabinets and furniture—a cross between my father and all the bearded young baristas my mother has befriended.

For months, it was my own past that I scoured this way, all the photographs of me and Emily, memories no longer belonging to the life I was living. Emily and I on a camping trip, though I hated camping. Emily and I taking surfing lessons. Had I even wanted to surf? If we'd spent our lives together, I would have said I enjoyed these things, even though I am quite happy never to set foot inside a wetsuit again.

In Jana's pictures she looks happy. She and her husband are always travelling and holding each other and posing for the camera. After another timeless stretch down the rabbit hole of her life, I surface to Douglas's home office full of binders and filing cabinets and neat stacks of paper. The house is still. I imagine my father is out in the kitchen, placing the cutting board on the counter, setting the oven, while my mother putters around him, every so often touching his shoulder, quoting some movie they watched together twenty-odd years ago. Perhaps my parents have sold their home and moved into this chic condominium. Perhaps they've won the lottery or inherited money from my mother's side of the family. Maybe they're living the life my mother always wanted them to live.

*

In the back of a Toronto taxi, I think of the last times Emily and I had sex. The licks and pressures, the breathless urging, the characters we'd slip into, all the words we'd barely acknowledge having spoken in the light of day—it had never slowed. In fact, the final few months had seemed notable as being particularly loving and physical. Perhaps she'd been wavering between extremes of love and disaffection, steeling herself for a day or two for her inevitable decision, before backtracking, realizing her mistake. Or maybe, looking from the outside, knowing it was over, she began seeing me the way she used to, back at the start.

I know the city well enough to sense we are getting close to the lake. At this hour, the main street of Jana's neighbourhood is sleepy with closed shops and quiet sidewalks, and the side streets have narrow brick houses with porches hidden behind the thick trunks of trees. The short lawns are sloped and tended but not fussed over. Life here looks crowded and harried and a touch raw. One corner lot is strewn with old, broken bits of furniture. And yet, behind the houses, I imagine tires hanging from branches, a sandbox with children's toys scattered around it, perhaps a small garden or a tree house—a place where lives are deeply rooted, long marriages in progress, children asleep in their beds.

In the back of the cab, I imagine calling my sister and explaining where I'm headed. It calms me somewhat when I begin to think of the entire escapade as a story I can tell. *Where did Jana live? What was the house like? Were the children there?* My initial conversation with Jana at the Halifax airport would have been enough to warrant a night's dissection between me and my sister, let alone the emails Jana and I exchanged, let alone whatever is to come.

"Guess who emailed me?" I told my mother as we came into the coffee shop this morning for a final visit.

She studied my face. I'd since confessed that the married woman I'd encountered on the flight was Jana.

"And?" she said coyly. She'd always tried impressing on her children that we could be open with her and that she could be a dispassionate arbiter of all our moral quandaries.

The plan was that Jana would meet me at the airport. I flew in near midnight and flew out at seven in the morning. A friend in Mississauga had been going to put me up, but now I was going to cancel with the friend so I could see Jana.

"This was her idea?" said my mother.

"She thought maybe we could get a drink someplace. I think because I complained about the bad schedule."

"Is there anything open in the airport in the middle of the night?"

I didn't know or much care. Jana's email had started an engine inside me and its sudden potential coloured everything. I could barely imagine what we'd say or do once we were together. I could hardly even picture her face now. Our meeting was surreal and precarious and I regretted bringing it up to my mother. It would have been one thing to replay it all after it had happened, but the whole magical scenario would likely dissolve if I looked too hard.

"Well," she said, and took a drink.

"Don't."

"What?"

"Don't ruin it."

"I always liked Jana," she said.

"Maybe she isn't married," I said, helplessly anticipating my mother's next question. "All I saw was on Facebook." I thought to note that there were plenty of pictures of me and Emily on my own account. Or maybe the man in the pictures was just a good friend who went on vacation with her. Or maybe the husband had been in an accident, had been struck by a car.

"She has children, though?" said my mother.

"Yes. Three."

"And you're prepared for three children?"

"We're meeting for a drink."

My mother widened her eyes and said maybe I was getting into more than I knew.

On the flight from Vancouver into Toronto, I couldn't help but see the possibility of my whole life stretched to fit some new, necessary form. If it got serious, would I leave my job? Jana was a pediatrician and two of her kids were in school, so it seemed sensible that I would be the one to pull up stakes. I'd gone to university in Toronto and always meant to return. Maybe I'd have better prospects. Or maybe I'd take some time and look after the girls and the house and whatever else Jana needed from me. For years, I'd been considering writing a book about Alice Munro. It was a short trip to Wingham, where Munro had grown up, and Clinton, where she'd lived in the decades after returning to Ontario after her first marriage ended. What would Munro think of a domesticated man, cleaning the dishes and minding the children while he revisited "Dulse" and "The Albanian Virgin"? Of course, I would be opting to live this life, wouldn't I? It would be my choice. As it stood, however, I could never afford to move. I had student loans, no benefits, no savings, a dying car, and a sessional job at a university that paid me less than the manager of a fast food restaurant.

As I was boarding my flight in Vancouver, Jana texted to ask if it really made sense to meet in the airport. *What do you think of just coming straight to my place? Adam is away visiting his parents.* I passed over that last part and pulled out of line to scribble her address down on a scrap of paper—in case my phone died, or got stolen, or was sucked out of the window of the plane.

*

One afternoon when I was sitting at the desk in Douglas's office and scrolling through Jana's life, an inbox notification appeared on my screen. I glanced down to find **Jana Ingram** displayed in bold letters and I instinctively backed my chair away. Without reading or even opening her email, I closed the window and snapped my computer shut. A confluence of guilt and coincidence gave way to terror as I imagined her message: *Please stop stalking me and my family!*

A year earlier, I'd had a similar sinking moment of feeling caught out. I was in my car preparing to make the drive to Moncton with the dog's ashes beside me. My mother was still in Mexico—I hadn't yet disclosed the news of Franklyn's death—and just as I began to back out of my driveway, I received a text from her: *Haven't heard from you. How's my sweet boy??*

The taxi stops abruptly. The street is otherwise empty. Without a word, the driver shifts and accelerates backwards. The night is silent and the rising pitch of the vehicle in reverse is like an alarm sounding. As the car comes to a rest, a mist hangs in the air, and the winter night feels disturbingly mild. I try to shut the door gently. I worry about waking Jana's children. After the driver hands me my suitcase, he slams the trunk down hard, and as he pulls away I glance at the dark windows of the neighbouring houses. At one in the morning, I've surely woken the entire street.

With the taxi gone, silence floods back. Nothing feels the way I imagined. I'm standing on a regular street with regular houses. Life never takes you to the places you picture in your head. I'd run through a million scenarios but never considered the possibility of never even seeing Jana. Now, the thought of just leaving crosses my mind. I could say my flight was delayed or that I'd misheard her address. I am still formulating these thoughts as I make my way up the walkway, lifting my suitcase across all its breaks and cracks, stepping up each of the stone steps. Under the portico at the top, I gaze through a tall rectangular window in the front door down a long, dark corridor. Soft light spills from a backroom at the far end, revealing hints of the warped hardwood before quickly giving way to black.

I knock. Jana is surely down there, reading or drinking or just waiting—perhaps the taxi hasn't made such a disturbance after all.

I search for some sign of movement and then knock again, a little louder, but not so loud that it would be heard by anyone asleep in their bed.

It isn't only the thought of those children that spooks me. A soiled green shovel with a long, sturdy wooden handle leans beside the front door next to a squat yellow bag of road salt torn open at the top. Maybe they have an arrangement, maybe Adam knows tonight is the night another man is visiting his wife.

I take a breath, staring a moment into the quiet home, before reaching for my phone, remembering that I shut it off on the flight. When it lights up, I find a flurry of messages.

—*Did you get my text?*

—*Mark, if you got that, let me know.*

—*Hi. Just checking if you got my message about meeting at my place.*

—*Okay, I'm going to stick with the first plan in case you didn't receive any of this! On my way!*

To my horror, I realize I never responded when she told me about meeting at her place. I received her message but never confirmed.

I leave my bags and wander down to the sidewalk to call. This moment and the morning back at my mother's seem a hundred years apart.

"Mark!" says Jana the instant she picks up. "I'm so sorry. Where are you?"

"No, it's my fault. I got your note and wrote down your address when I was boarding, but I never—"

"So you're at my place?"

"I was just standing on your front porch."

"Okay. Go around the back and you'll see three flowerpots on a little stand beneath the window. The key is there under the middle one. You can just let yourself in and I'll be there soon."

I begin to ask about her kids, and she tells me that nobody is home. The kids are with their father.

"I'm so sorry! I should have been there. I've been staying at a friend's, and it just seemed easier to come and meet you. I thought I was being extra careful. I didn't want you to get lost—I didn't want to miss you."

"It's my fault," I say again.

"Mark, I really want to see you." She says this in a tone that makes everything clear.

Turning the key and pushing the side door of Jana's home open into darkness, I feel like someone is watching me. I know I'm not breaking in and that the house is empty and yet I close the door as gently as possible, and then, thinking better, I reopen it and shut it a fraction harder, more naturally, a proclamation of innocence.

"Hello?" I say, with less force than I intended. I search for a light, but once I feel the switch on my finger I hesitate, listening to the silence, breathing in the strong scent of leather above a hint of earth and moss and old wood.

As my eyes adjust, I notice a huddle of criss-crossed skis in the corner, what looks like a large bird feeder, and at my feet dozens of pairs of little shoes.

Crossing the hallway, I peer towards the front entrance with the tall window where I was just standing, outside looking in. Now I know that it's the kitchen where the light is on. There's a lamp on a stone ledge tucked in behind a wide oak table, illuminating a cluttered shelf of assorted books and games: Toni Morrison, Risk, a beaten-up Hungry Hippos, Michael Crichton, Ursula Le Guin. The books are standing or leaning or toppled over, the floor is dark wood and uneven and very heavy-looking. The whole scene feels like a mystery I'm meant to solve.

I pull out a chair without making a sound. There's a hum from the refrigerator, a faint clanking from a hot water radiator.

On the counter, various shades and colours of tea leaves reside in glass containers beside an old letterpress tray holding a wall of spices, all fastidiously arranged and labelled with the odd piece missing: *tumer c*, *regano*, *coriand*. Cast iron pots and pans hang from hooks. Everything is organized and yet at the point of bursting like an apothecary with more jars than shelves.

In the stillness, I feel a skittish thrill for what awaits me. Will we sit here and talk when she arrives? Will we go straight to her bedroom? How will it all happen? What words will we use?

A week ago, if I'd been dropped into this moment, what would I have made of it? I've sometimes taken pleasure in my ability to deduce a password for an account I haven't used in ages—I will think *Where was I living? What was I reading?* Standing in Jana's kitchen, I envision my past self—the one from only a week ago—rooting through the cupboards and closets, peering out the windows, trying to make sense of this future moment.

A year ago, what would I have made of that Vancouver condo with its voice-operated flat-screen television? Five years ago, what would I have made of my entire existence in the absence of my father? Of finding all those photographs of Emily and Mark?

A noise startles me to attention. I slap my thigh instinctively before understanding, then free my phone from my jeans.

On my way! reads the text. *You get in all right?*

Yep, I write. *In the kitchen.*

Awaiting her reply, I sense a presence hovering in the unlit corridor. At first the presence is a hint of movement and then a dark, ghostly shape cut out of the grey-white wall.

"Hello?" the ghost says, flatly, without the least concern. It is the voice of a child who might have been expecting to come downstairs to find a stranger in her home.

My phone chimes again and the girl's eyes follow the sound.

"It's your mother," I say slowly, awaiting the girl's reaction, my heart hammering, hoping this will put her at ease.

The girl doesn't do or say anything. She might be ten or eleven, her hair in tangles on her shoulders, her eyes wide apart like her mother's, her bare feet so pale they are almost glowing against the dark wood.

"Are you Mia?" I ask, just as I realize from her faraway look that she is not fully conscious, aware of me only as a man in a dream.

"Mia?" says a man's voice slicing through the dark.

I hear footsteps on the staircase, the creak and moan of century-old wood.

I think to run, but instead I brace myself for violence, staring hard into the black for a figure to emerge.

"I'm Mark, Luke's friend," I say the second I see motion. "I have a key. Jana thought the house would be empty."

Her husband is shorter than I expected. He has a high forehead and a wide bare chest. He reaches for his daughter and swings her up over his shoulder in one smooth motion.

I expect an interrogation about Jana's instructions, about how long it is I'm staying, about how I know Luke. I must seem to him like a desperate man in search of shelter.

"She could have left you some sheets," is all he says, leading me into a room at the front of the house. He flicks on a lamp that is the Eiffel Tower with a cream-coloured shade over it. After returning from upstairs, he lays out my bedding, which smells faintly of vomit, and a pillow so soft it can't keep its shape. Finally, he points out a throw blanket on a trunk by the window.

I thank him and expect he'll return to bed, but he lingers,

watching as I spread the covers onto the sofa and arrange the blanket. Only when I get myself settled, fully clothed, do I hear the sound of his footsteps on the stairs.

Closing my eyes, a wave of exhaustion washes over me, and I picture myself on a raft in some black and endless ocean. Then, I think of Luke in his jogging pants, pushing his cart through the aisles of the grocery store, nodding hello to all our former teachers and hockey coaches, all the parents of his ex-girlfriends. It seems only a moment later that my alarm rumbles in my pocket, meaning hours have passed.

Frozen in the darkness, I realize I never texted Jana to tell her about her husband, and if she came in, I never heard her. I reason that her husband must have phoned her to say Luke's friend had arrived and he was set up on the sofa. Or, more likely, he saw straight through my story and called to mock or condemn her: *Your man is on the sofa. I gave him a used pillowcase from the hamper and the sheets that the baby puked on.*

Ian Williams

―――――

BRO

Greg was on a mission to make a Black friend but there weren't many, any, Black people where he lived.

He made this declaration upon awaking one morning from uneasy dreams (he was chasing a man), his head hanging off the left side of the bed, his lower back stiff. He could hear his wife typing at her improvised workstation in the closet.

When he repeated his goal, his wife admonished him that he should not approach finding a Black friend as an item on a check-list, or collecting rare Pokémon, or harpooning a white whale.

It's a person you're talking about, she said. Not a deer head for the wall.

Of course, he said. (The man was on foot. Greg was in his truck.) Why would she think— He liked Black people. He felt sorry for them, especially after those killings in America a few years ago.

Tragic, he said. He rolled out of the bed onto his knees. Just tragic.

Greg, honey, I'm about to enter a meeting.

What can we do about it? He was resurrecting an old conversation.

Nothing, she said before realizing that the question, this time, was not rhetorical. I mean, donate. Every day there's someone on my Facebook suggesting an organization.

I don't want to give money. I want to *do* something.

Giving money is doing something. She turned on the ring light. I'm signing in.

I'm not giving money so some bureaucrat could write off his lunch, he said, although corporate fraud didn't strike him as something Black people did.

Then do whatever. Move to Toronto and make all the Black friends you want. Go to Africa. Then she put on her professional voice and began greeting her colleagues and he had to crawl out of the room so he wouldn't appear half-naked in the background of her Zoom call.

*

Not counting the NBA, he saw very few, no, Black people on a daily basis. To his knowledge, his wife didn't have any Black friends either, not even on Facebook. (The man in the dream was illuminated by Greg's headlights. The hair along the back of his neck was like peppercorn.) So when he beheld a Black man at the Home Depot in the next town, he recognized the significance of the occasion. The man was in a navy-blue uniform, standing inside the automatic doors. He was one of those new security guards hired by the store to count capacity limits and urge customers toward the sanitizer.

Greg didn't know how to talk to the man. All his lines seemed like pickup lines, since, before getting married, he had ever only thought about approaching women. He would have to build this friendship in stages.

On the way in, he nodded at the man.

On the way out, holding a shovel, he said, Bro, and made a fist in his coat pocket but chickened out of raising it in a fight-the-power, 1960s-Olympics way. Black Panther way. That guy from *Black Panther* who died. Tragic. Just tragic. Colon cancer.

Stage 1 complete.

*

I made a Black friend, Greg announced to his wife.

Checkmark, she said.

He deposited the shovel in the foyer and unlaced his boots.

What's his name?

Before Greg could recall or fabricate a name (the man in the dream owed him something and was trying to escape), his wife made a smug, knowing sound.

I'm not good with names, he said. He remembered noticing a name tag and company logo stitched on the Black man's uniform.

Labels. She finger-quoted to mock him. Do you even know my name, Greg?

Male friendships aren't like female friendships, he said.

His wife scraped the price tag from the handle of the shovel with a fingernail.

Guys don't really care about names, Greg went on. I call him Bro.

*

He couldn't risk losing Bro to shift schedules, so he drove back to Home Depot that night through freezing rain for stage 2.

He entered, seemingly absorbed on his phone.

You're missing a hell of a game, he said as he approached Bro.

Bro said nothing for a long second and Greg thought he might have miscalculated the interest Black men have in basketball.

It's close, Greg said, as cool as possible. But Toronto's up by three.

Bro looked around then something in him relaxed. (Eventually he cornered the man in an alley.)

I'm tracking the score right here, he said, and patted the phone in his breast pocket, over his heart, a gesture that seemed both patriotic and affectionate.

From that point, it was a smooth ride through stages 3, 4, 5, and 6 to besties. Greg told the man about his sixty-five-inch TV, bet him money that the Raptors would make the playoffs, invited him over to the house, texted his address as a way of getting Bro's number. Greg didn't stop talking until a voice overhead said, Attention shoppers, the store is now closing.

We're vaxxed and boostered, so seriously, drop by any time once you see my truck in the driveway.

Careful what you wish for, Bro said.

They bumped elbows. Greg grabbed some rock salt and furnace filters on sale then checked out.

Keep it real, Bro, Greg said at the exit, and flicked a peace sign.

In his truck, he opened his contacts and saved his new friend's number under *Bro*.

*

Greg stopped parking in the garage. He left his truck in the driveway. (The man was blocked by the car on one side and a chain-link fence on the other.) Left the porch light on all night. He agonized over when and how much to text Bro. Bro responded with GIFs and emojis. Black thumbs-up. Black happy faces. He called twice but Bro didn't pick up. *Sorry, was working,* Bro texted.

Greg didn't lose hope that Bro would accept his invitation one day, but in the meantime, he kept looking for other Black-friend candidates. He followed Black athletes, Black comedians, a Black meteorologist from TV, he friended the Black friends of friends. He drew the line at a Black politician he despised, who knotted his scarf in an affected way that irked Greg. He didn't have to like someone just because they were Black.

But his thoughts kept returning to Bro. When he tried to visualize the kind of Black friend he wanted, he could only come up with minor variations of Bro. Even Bro's youth didn't bother him. They could watch TV on the couch with a bowl of chips between them. Greg could dole out fatherly advice about Bro's ex-girlfriend who had started dating someone else. They could score women on a scale of one to ten, face and body categories, as they appeared onscreen. They could rewind the nude scenes on Netflix.

*

On another Bro-less winter evening, while Greg was watching basketball and sinking into a funk, his wife looked at him, exhaled, and said, You know, I'm part Black.

It was the fourth quarter. She was on the far end of the couch. He had trouble reading her face in the dark after drinking a few beers. She folded the arms of her reading glasses and placed them on the coffee table.

How? he asked. (He remembered thinking in the dream that he had to act quickly or the man would jump over the fence.) He couldn't focus. He muted the TV. (Greg got out of the car and approached the man.) How Black?

Small. Fractional, she said. How is one to know those things, Greg? How Italian are you?

One-eighth, he said.

Well, I don't know. The relative—

Ancestor. That's their preferred word.

She didn't take his correction. —is on my mom's side, but nobody really talks about it. His wife explained that before her sister died of leukemia, she spent a lot of time researching the family lineage so she could leave something to her children. Her AncestryDNA test turned up some Black blood.

That's great, Greg said. A three-pointer caught his eye. That's unbelievable.

*

The next morning, despite a slight headache, Greg went to work in his wife's closet office. He could hear her moving around the room, asking no questions despite his very intriguing posture of a philosopher: writing in a notebook with one hand and eating an apple with the other.

I've planned what I'm going to do, he said.

I need this space, Greg. She was groomed from the shoulders up, inserting an earring into her right ear.

I'm organizing a protest.

She let her arms fall to her side.

A Black Lives Matter protest, he explained.

But why?

For Black solidarity or—what's the word?—allyship.

Yes, but, Greg, protests usually are in response to something.

She adopted the patient voice she used when onboarding new employees. You protest *against* something. Something specific. No one got shot recently.

No one you know about.

There was no verdict on the news.

Doesn't need to be. I'm protesting everything, baby. Slavery, the police, the criminal justice system, Karens, Katrina, the war on drugs, Mandela—

You're protesting Mandela?

All that lost time, how they treated Obama, the banana thing in Italy, that syphilis thing in Tennessee,

I don't think you know what you're talking about.

Blood diamonds, the Congo mines for electric cars—I'm protesting all of it.

His wife was frowning deeply. Maybe you should talk to Bro before doing anything.

I already messaged him. He's down. Greg recalled Bro's thumbs-up emoji of support. I told him that you were Black. He had no idea.

Don't tell people I'm Black. I'm not Black.

You are. It's nothing to be ashamed about.

I'm not!

Greg wasn't sure which, Black or ashamed.

I'm not, his wife continued, in any real sense. People don't become Black just like that.

What you're feeling now is forty-three years of white privilege. He didn't intend to sound patronizing. But that doesn't mean you can't claim your heritage.

What heritage? Look at me! She was wearing a blazer and a silk scarf on top but checkered pajama pants and slippers below.

My sister—God bless her soul—found some info in a forum online and suddenly I'm supposed to wear a kente head wrap so you could go around saying you have a Black wife?

Greg recalled the hair products she used to control frizz in the summer.

So you could check a census box? So you could legitimize whatever self-righteous idea is your latest passion project? She was shouting now. You're white, Greg. You're a forty-four-year-old white man. Those people have nothing to do with your life.

Greg looked down at his protest notes from the morning.

I mean, they're important but—

But what?

Just but. She turned on the ring light. I have a meeting and you're in my chair. This is my space.

*

Greg scheduled the protest for a Sunday afternoon in front of the town hall. But the main entrance was cordoned off for construction, so he quickly had to relocate the protest to another entrance—the public library entrance.

Why not protest *Huckleberry Finn* while you're at it? his wife said. As far as he could tell, she was there to atone for her outburst, but Greg hoped the protest would connect her to her inner Blackness, a phrase that caused her to roll her eyes whenever he said it.

He snapped a photo of the location and sent it to Bro. (In the dream, the man looked between Greg and the chain-link fence.)

The protesters comprised four high-schoolers and Greg. Nobody had a bullhorn. One student began creating a sign on the spot by ripping a sheet out of her notebook and writing the letters *BLM* in marker but Greg said, No words. As he was outlining the choreography of the protest, he caught his wife looking at the group with her head tilted as if trying to read vertical text.

I called the news crews, he said.

Oh, sweet heavens, no, his wife said. She pulled a pair of sunglasses out of her bag and walked toward the construction vehicles.

Keep an eye out for Bro, he called after her, then turned back to the protesters. Direct all media questions to me.

The students nodded. The five protesters took their seats on the steps of the library. They all wore black as Greg had instructed on Facebook. He distributed the masks that he bought online—black with a white fist on the front—and the students giggled.

According to Greg's notebook, the protest was in the tradition of the non-verbal/sit-in/occupy sort. It looked, at first, like performance art. About fifteen minutes in, when the initial excitement wore off and a few protesters were sitting with their eyes closed in the drizzle, it looked more like Falun Gong meditation. Then after another fifteen minutes, the students started checking their phones and the protest simply looked like a father and his four kids waiting for a minivan.

Greg checked his phone. Rain splattered on his screen. No notifications from Bro. No activity on the Facebook event page.

After an hour, his wife returned. Okay that's enough. Do any of you kids need a ride?

More people will join us, Greg said.

Bro is not coming. She delivered the statement bluntly, as an atheist would to a believer.

Yet as they were speaking, the eyes of the students focused on something in the distance. (In the dream, the man ran toward the fence.) When Greg looked, he saw a Black man walking toward the group. (Through the fence. It sliced diamonds through his body as he crossed yet he emerged intact on the other side.) His wife's mouth hung open.

Greg stood up to greet him.

Sorry, the man said. There was a parade I had to cover. He looked around as if trying to determine whether he had missed the protest. I write for *The Trend*. Are you Greg?

I am. Greg stretched his lower back and looked both weary and mildly heroic, one foot on the sidewalk, one on a step, the slightest lift of his chin.

Cool, cool. I was expecting a brotha—

He's tied up.

Cool, cool. The man tapped his phone a few times and held it under Greg's mouth. So, tell me, Greg, why are you doing this?

*

Greg read the article to his wife from his phone while lying in bed. The article had quoted him as saying "centuries of oppression," "systemic racism," "call to action for every citizen."

I'm going to send the link to Bro, he said.

Oh, Greg, honey. Please don't.

He hadn't heard from Bro in a while. That man worked too much. (And the man kept running through a field on the other side of the fence without looking back to see if Greg was still chasing him or not.)

I mean, you've done enough. His wife turned away from him. So much already.

CONTRIBUTORS' BIOGRAPHIES

MADHUR ANAND is a writer and a scientist. Her debut book of prose, the experimental memoir-in-parts *This Red Line Goes Straight to Your Heart* (Strange Light, 2020), won the Governor General's Literary Award for Nonfiction. Her debut collection of poems *A New Index for Predicting Catastrophes* (McClelland & Stewart, 2015) was a finalist for the Trillium Book Award for Poetry, was named one of ten all-time "trailblazing" poetry collections by the CBC, and received a starred review in *Publishers Weekly*. Her second collection of poems *Parasitic Oscillations* (McClelland & Stewart, 2022) was also a finalist for the Trillium Book Award for Poetry, and was named a *Globe and Mail* Top 100 Book and a "top pick" for Spring poetry by the CBC. She is working on a novel. She is a Professor of Ecology and Sustainability at the University of Guelph, where she was appointed the inaugural Director of the Guelph Institute for Environmental Research.

SHARON BALA's bestselling debut novel, *The Boat People* (McClelland & Stewart, 2018), won the 2020 Newfoundland & Labrador Book Award and the 2019 Harper Lee Prize for Legal Fiction. It was a finalist for Canada Reads 2018, the 2018 Amazon Canada First Novel Award, the Margaret and John Savage First Book Award, and the Thomas Raddall Atlantic Fiction Award, and was longlisted for the International Dublin Literary Award and the Aspen Words Literary Prize. *The Boat People* is on sale worldwide, with translations in French, German, Arabic, and Turkish.

In 2017 Sharon won the Writers' Trust/McClelland & Stewart Journey Prize. Her short fiction has appeared in: *Hazlitt, Grain, PRISM international, The Dalhousie Review, The New Quarterly, Maisonneuve, Joyland, Room,* and *Riddle Fence.*

Sharon is a member of The Port Authority, a St John's writing group. In 2015 they published a short story collection called *Racket* with Breakwater Books. She's currently working on a second novel and writing a play. Visit her online at: sharonbala.com.

GARY BARWIN is a writer, composer, and multidisciplinary artist and the author of thirty books, including *Nothing the Same, Everything Haunted: The Ballad of Motl the Cowboy* (Vintage Canada, 2022), which won the Canadian Jewish Literary Award and was chosen for Hamilton Reads 2023. His national bestselling novel *Yiddish for Pirates* (Vintage Canada, 2016) won the Leacock Medal for Humour and the Canadian Jewish Literary Award, was a finalist for the Governor General's Award for Fiction and the Scotiabank Giller Prize, and was longlisted for Canada Reads. His latest book is *Imagining Imagining: Essays on Language, Identity and Infinity* published in Fall 2023. Born in Northern Ireland to South African parents of Lithuanian Ash-

kenazi descent, he lives in Hamilton, Ontario, Canada. garybarwin.
com

BILLY-RAY BELCOURT is a writer from the Driftpile Cree
Nation. He is an Assistant Professor in the School of Creative
Writing at the University of British Columbia. He is the author
of four books: *This Wound is a World* (Frontenac House, 2019),
NDN Coping Mechanisms: Notes from the Field (House of Anansi,
2019), *A History of My Brief Body* (Penguin Canada, 2021), and *A
Minor Chorus* (Hamish Hamilton, 2022).

Born and raised in Jamaica, XAIVER MICHAEL CAMPBELL has
considered Newfoundland and Labrador home for over a decade. These islands are quite different, but Xaiver feels that living
in Jamaica prepared him for life on the Rock. Minus the snow,
sleet, and lack of sun—the people are equally warm and friendly.
When not writing, doing childcare, baking, playing, or watching
basketball, Xaiver loves the outdoors and can be found swimming in the ponds all across Newfoundland in the summer,
camping and hiking the East Coast Trail.

His fiction has been published in *The Malahat Review, Riddle
Fence,* and the anthologies *Us, Now* and *Hard Ticket* by Breakwater Books and *Release Any Words Stuck Inside You III* by
Applebeard Editions. His second play, *One Name,* was produced
by Halifax Theatre for Young People in spring 2023. Xaiver's
non-fiction work concerns the lives of enslaved and freed Black
people in early Newfoundland settlements. His first non-fiction
book, *Black Harbour,* forthcoming Fall 2023, offers an introduc-
tion to Newfoundland Black history. Xaiver was named a Writer's
Trust Rising Star in 2022.

CORINNA CHONG's first novel, *Belinda's Rings,* was published by NeWest Press in 2013, and her reviews and short fiction have appeared in magazines across Canada. She won the 2021 CBC Short Story Prize for "Kids in Kindergarten." *The Whole Animal,* a collection of short stories, was published by Arsenal Pulp Press in April 2023. She lives in Kelowna, BC, and teaches at Okanagan College.

BETH DOWNEY is an emerging writer across creative disciplines. Her work has recently appeared in *The New Quarterly* and Riddle Fence Magazine. In 2023 Beth was awarded The Word Guild's Wendy Elaine Nelles Memorial Prize for developing writers. She has contributed editorially to published works in poetry and prose, recently including Terry Doyle's *Dig* (Breakwater, 2019.) A diaspora Newfoundlander, Beth currently divides life between Winnipeg and St John's teaching, parenting, and completing doctoral work in English Literature. She moonlights as a childbirth doula.

ALLISON GRAVES received her BA in English Literature from Dalhousie University and her MA in Creative Writing from Memorial University, where she wrote a collection of short stories called *Soft Serve*—forthcoming this September with Breakwater Books. Her fiction has won *Room Magazine*'s annual fiction contest and the Newfoundland Arts and Letters Award. She is the current fiction editor of *Riddle Fence,* Newfoundland's Journal of Arts and Culture. She is doing a PhD at Memorial and teaches in the English Department.

JOEL THOMAS HYNES is a writer and performer from Calvert, Newfoundland. He has authored numerous books, stage plays, and feature films and is the creator of the award-winning CBC comedy series *Little Dog*. His most recent novel, *We'll All Be Burnt in Our Beds Some Night* (Harper Perennial, 2017), won the Governor General's Award for Fiction, the BMO Winterset Award, and the NL Writer's Alliance Award for Fiction. *Cast No Shadow,* the feature film adaptation of his novella *Say Nothing Saw Wood* (Running the Goat, 2013) (which was also adapted to stage) won Hynes the award for Best Atlantic Screenwriter at FINN and was nominated for a Canadian Screen Award for Best Adapted Screenplay. As an actor JTH has held lead and principal roles for numerous films and TV series, including *Down to the Dirt, Republic of Doyle, Cast No Shadow, A Small Fortune, Orphan Black, Little Dog, Book of Negroes,* and *Trickster.* He is a graduate of the Canadian Film Centre's Screenwriter's Lab and holds an MFA in Creative Nonfiction from University of King's College, Halifax. Also a musician, Hynes's most recent studio album *Dead Man's Melody* is available across all online platforms including Apple Music and Spotify. Hynes lives in St John's, Newfoundland.

ELISE LEVINE is the author of *Say This: Two Novellas* (Biblioasis, 2022), the story collections *This Wicked Tongue* (Biblioasis, 2019) and *Driving Men Mad* (Emblem Editions, 2003), and the novels *Blue Field* (Biblioasis, 2017) and *Requests and Dedications* (Emblem Editions, 2005). Her work has also appeared or is forthcoming in publications including *The Walrus, The Hopkins Review, Ploughshares, Blackbird, The Gettysburg Review,* and *Best Canadian Stories.* Originally from Toronto, she lives in Baltimore, where she teaches in the MA in Writing program at Johns Hopkins University.

Dr SOURAYAN MOOKERJEA is Research Director of the Intermedia Research Studio and Professor of Sociology at University of

Alberta, in Treaty Six Territory, where he specializes in intermedia research-creation, critical social and intermedia theory, global sociology, political ecology, and energy humanities. His poetry and research-creation probes include contributions to publications, interventions, and exhibitions such as: *(Re)Markable Time* (University of Alberta, 2013), *Alleyways: Capillaries of Urban Living* (University of Alberta, 2014), *In-Toxic* (Latitude 53, 2016), *TranscUlturAl* (2016), *Polyglot Magazine of Poetry and Art* (2017), *Prototypes for Possible Worlds* (FAB Gallery, 2019), *Seed Time* (2019), *Seed Time Squared* (2022), the *Energy Emergency Repair Kit/UnPacking Energy Transitions* (The Square, St Gallen, 2022), and *The Institution of Knowledge* (FAB Gallery, 2023). His research addresses questions of ecological and climate debt, environmental racism, and the cultural and class politics of renewable energy system change. He is co-director of *Toxic Media Ecologies: Critical Responses to the Cultural Politics of Planetary Crisis; Feminist Energy Futures: Powershift and Environmental Social Justice;* and *iDoc: Intermedia and Documentary;* as well as a co-investigator on the research-creation collaboration *Speculative Energy Futures.* He was Kule Scholar of Climate Resilience (2020–23).

LUE PALMER is a writer of prose and poetry on Black relationships to nature, the fantastic in the everyday, and the retelling of history. They have roots in Portland, Jamaica, and are currently at work on their first novel, *The Hungry River.* Lue is beginning a new facet of their career in climate work, writing about environmental racism. They were a recipient of the 2021 Octavia E. Butler Memorial Scholarship, an alumni of the Clarion West Program, and a recent graduate of Columbia University Graduate School of Journalism.

MICHELLE PORTER is a writer originally from the Métis prairie homeland. She is the descendant of a long line of Métis storytellers (the Goulet family). Her first novel, *A Grandmother Begins the Story* (Viking), was published in May 2023. She is the author of two books of non-fiction, *Approaching Fire* (Breakwater Books, 2020) and *Scratching River* (Wilfrid Laurier University Press, 2022), and one book of poetry, *Inquiries* (Breakwater Books, 2019). She lives in Newfoundland and Labrador and teaches creative writing at Memorial University.

SARA POWER is a storyteller from Labrador and a former artillery officer in the Canadian Forces. In 2022, she was a finalist for the RBC/PEN Canada New Voices Award and a nominee for a National Magazine Award. Her short fiction won *The Malahat Review*'s 2022 Open Season Award and *Riddle Fence*'s Fiction Award, and placed second in the *Toronto Star* Short Story Contest. Her debut collection of short fiction, *Art of Camouflage,* is forthcoming with Freehand Books in 2024. She currently lives in Ottawa with her husband, three children, and a coonhound.

RYAN TURNER's stories have been published in magazines such as *The New Quarterly, The Ex-Puritan,* and *Prairie Fire.* He's published two short story collections and both were shortlisted for the ReLit Award. His latest book, *Half-Sisters & Other Stories,* was published by Gaspereau Press in 2019. He is the co-founder and co-director of the AfterWords Literary Festival in Halifax.

IAN WILLIAMS is the author of the novel *Reproduction,* which was the winner of the 2019 Scotiabank Giller Prize and was published in the US, UK, and Italy; *Personals,* which was shortlisted for the Griffin Poetry Prize and the Robert Kroetsch Poetry Book Award; *Not Anyone's Anything*, winner of the Danuta Gleed Literary Award for the best first collection of short fiction in Canada, and *You Know Who You Are*, a finalist for the ReLit Prize for poetry. In 2020 he published his latest poetry collection, *Word Problems*. In fall 2021 he released *Disorientation: The Experience of Being Black in the World*, which was shortlisted for the Hilary Weston Writers Trust Prize for Non-Fiction and the BC Book Prize for Non-Fiction. Williams is Associate Professor of English at the University of Toronto and Director of the Creative Writing Program. He is currently on the board of the Griffin Poetry Prize. Born in Trinidad, Williams grew up in Brampton, Ontario, and has worked in Massachusetts and Ontario.

PUBLICATIONS CONSULTED FOR THE 2024 EDITION

For the 2024 edition of *Best Canadian Stories*, the following publications were consulted:

The Antigonish Review, Border Crossings, Broken Pencil, Canadian Notes & Queries, Carte Blanche, Catapult, The Dalhousie Review, Electric Literature, EVENT, *The Ex-Puritan, Exile Quarterly, The Fiddlehead, filling Station, Freefall, Geist, Grain, Granta, Hazlitt, The Hong Kong Review, The Humber Literary Review, Hypertext Magazine, Joyland, Leaf Magazine, Maisonneuve, The Malahat Review, Maple Tree Literary Supplement, The Massachussets Review, Minola Review, The Moth, Narrative Magazine, The Nashwaak Review, The New Quarterly, Open Minds Quarterly, paperplates, Parentheses Journal, The Paris Review, Plenitude, Prairie Fire,* PRISM *International, The Quarantine Review, Queen's Quarterly, Qwerty Magazine, Room, subTerrain, Taddle Creek, The / temz / Review,* THIS *Magazine, The Threepenny Review, Uncanny Magazine, Understorey Magazine, The Walrus, The Windsor Review, WordCity Literary Journal, Zoetrope*

ACKNOWLEDGEMENTS

"Insects Eat Birds" by Madhur Anand was previously unpublished. Printed with permission of the author.

"Interloper" by Sharon Bala was previously unpublished. Printed with permission of the author.

"Golemson" by Gary Barwin first appeared in *Taddle Creek*. Reprinted with permission of the author.

"One Woman's Memories" by Billy-Ray Belcourt first appeared in *Maisonneuve*. Reprinted with permission of the author.

"Pitfalls of Unsolicited Shoulding" by Xaiver Michael Campbell was previously unpublished. Printed with permission of the author.

"Love Cream Heat" by Corinna Chong first appeared in *The Fiddlehead*. Reprinted with permission from *The Whole Animal* by Corinna Chong (Arsenal Pulp Press, 2023).

"The Bee Garden" by Beth Downey was previously unpublished. Printed with permission of the author.

EDITOR'S BIOGRAPHY

LISA MOORE's books have won the Commonwealth Writers' Prize and CBC's Canada Reads, been finalists for the Writers' Trust Fiction Prize and the Scotiabank Giller Prize, and been longlisted for the Booker Prize. She lives in St John's, Newfoundland.

Printed by Imprimerie Gauvin
Gatineau, Québec